THE TRUTH AND THE LIFE

Elizabeth Moore

Alternative Book Press
2 Timber Lane
Suite 301
Marlboro, NJ 07746
www.alternativebookpress.com

This is a work of fiction. All characters appearing in this work are fictitious. Any resemblance to real people, living or dead or otherwise, or locales is purely coincidental.

Excerpt from "Fire in the Pines" THE PINE BARRENS by John McPhee. Copyright © 1967, 1968 by John McPhee. Reprinted by permission of Farrar, Straus and Giroux, LLC

Publication Data
Elizabeth, Moore, [2014]
The Truth and The Life/ by Elizabeth Moore—1st ed.
p. cm.
1. General (Fiction). I Title.
PS1-3576.E45M667   2014
813'.6—dc23

ISBN 978-1-940122-20-5
Printed in the United States of America
10 9 8 7 6 5 4 3 2 1

Acknowledgements

Cedar Mill and its residents are fictional. One of my intentions in writing, however, was to portray a late nineteenth-century Pine Barrens town that might have reasonably existed. Among other local historical writings, I am indebted to William McMahon's <u>South Jersey Towns</u> and Henry Carlton Beck's <u>Forgotten Towns of Southern New Jersey</u> (Rutgers University Press, 1973 and 1983, respectively), whose portraits of the early industrial Pinelands towns—particularly the abandoned papermaking town of Harrisville—first provided the inspiration for what would ultimately become Cedar Mill. I am also thankful for the ongoing preservation and educational efforts at the present historic site of Batsto Village in New Jersey's Wharton State Forest, whose exhibits were particularly helpful to me in recounting some of the more "ordinary" details of village life in this period. In writing the dialogue, I was fortunate to be able to refer frequently to an extensive contemporary listing of local phrases and figures of speech ("Jerseyisms") in the American Dialect Society's <u>Dialect Notes, Volume I</u>, first printed in 1896.

This story is dedicated to my father, whose work to preserve and protect the New Jersey Pine Barrens first made it possible.

There has been so much fire in the pines for so many centuries that, through the resulting processes of natural selection, the species that grow there are not only highly flammable but are able to tolerate fire and come back quickly.

John McPhee, <u>The Pine Barrens</u>

Rachel

I'm settin in the cripple when I first hear the noise.

I'm hiding under the cedar trees and around the edge of the stable I can hear it just behind the mules stamping in their stalls. I sit there listening and every bit of me tingling. Then the noise stops. Pretty soon I hear Rebecca calling for me so I go on back to the store.

I'll be safe there cause she don't know. Only Joseph found us and I reckon that's over and done with. So I go in through the oak door in the back and sneak by the wall to the little kitchen behind the counter, where I can hear the old iron pot creaking and boiling away on the stove.

"There yare", Rebecca says. "Git to the dishes like I told you. The woods aint goin nowhare."

"The whippoorwill shoes're out an I wanna see."

"Don't you try me. You know what I'll do if I ketch you out thare looking for lady slippers when you know you aint supposed to be anywhare but here. Now git to the dishes like I told you."

I go around the back to the little tub while Rebecca stays out at the counter. Pretty soon Missus Cranmer comes in to buy a yard of calico and I watch till Rebecca goes to wait on her. When I'm sure no one's looking I take the huckleberries outta my dress pocket. I stand there holding them on my tongue, scrubbing and scrubbing.

After supper we're all outside runnin round behind Mister Hawthorne's garden patch. The trees are dry and a little tired-looking and the early summer air is heavy and still. I think about going back to the bog but Rebecca's still watching me from the store window, so instead I sit down on the ground and start braiding leaves of grass together and looking around for David. When Abigail sits next to me the air is growing cool around our heads. I dint think she'd ever wanna talk to me again after the bees.

"Saw you lookin for them burries," she says. She's picking at the grass too like she's had it in her mind the whole time. "Next time you should git some for me. Yer always snoopin in the woods and you never git any cept for yerself."

"Well I don't wanna git ketched. It's hard enough hidin a couple."

When Abigail leans in her head smells like the stable, all warm and sweet and blonde. "If you git me a couple tonight I'll show you whare the cave is," she says.

I think about that for a minute. That Abigail would ever of been brave enough to go looking for it is downright dubersome, to tell you the truth. Not without David or Joshua or one-a the other boys with her. So I tell her I don't believe her. Then I tell her to get lost.

"I promise!" She reaches for my hand. "It was me that found it."

I try to pull my hand away. "Naw, I think yer too afeared."

"I beant afeared! An guess what else—thare was bones in thare."

I have to admit I'd like to see them bones so I

sit there and think about it for awhile.

"If you bringum tonight and leavum under my bed I'll show you whare it is tomarra," she says.

I keep settin there thinking about it as she holds and holds my hand, right up until the warm stars begin to pop out and Rebecca calls us all to go on home.

After Pa's asleep, I climb up outta my blanket and go barefoot past the edge of his bed and so softly open the door. Outside I see Abigail's house across the mossy way. The little kerosene lamp in her window is still burning just a little, always lit since she's afeared of the dark and the woods. I can almost make out the mop of her head through the window. The moon is just barely out and the stars are hushed with clouds. Over in the cedars the crickets and the tree frogs are going loud and strong, creaking fastly like little rocking chairs.

I go like a shadow over the packed dirt of the road and turn off toward the barn and the cripple where the ground gets soft and springy and hollow-sounding. Then I creep between the sappy trunks and over the moss until I find the bush that's farthest from the stable and the road. It's the smallest one and the berries are scrawny and wrinkled. Lord knows I wanna see them bones but I still don't really like Abigail all that much.

As I reach in to grab the berries, a hand shoots down from a branch above and closes on my wrist like a dog's jaw. I have to bite on my tongue to keep quiet. That's when I see him hovering right over me there in the needles, his hair all dark and moon-shiny. I try and fight but David's a boy and older.

"Hushup," he says, then louder as I fight him, "hushup! Hushup!"

"Why you here?" I whisper-shout back. "They'll git you again. They'll git bothovus."

"Wouldn't that be somethin," he says. There's a look on his face I can see even in the dark, something so angry and triumphant in them pretty blue eyes. I know he's here cause he wants to get back at me for earlier.

"Aint my fault they ketched you steada me. You shouldn'ta had so much. Then you coulda run when you shoulda."

"They wouldn'ta ketched no one if you dint go an drop it," he says. "So now I'm gon give you what Joseph gave me."

He leaps down quick as a cat from the branch he's squatting on, and afore long we're settin beneath the tree on a bed of spragnum moss and he has me pulled her over his lap with his one hand holding me there while the other works at his belt buckle. "I'll show you," he mumbles again and again as he pulls the belt free and starts lifting my nightgown. Suddenly I want to cry out from the shame of it—that he's gone and honey-fogled me and ketched me here in the middle of the night and that now he's going to hit me and I'm naked under my nightgown and I know he can see it looking down at me. "You bastard. I'll git you. I'll tell Rebecca and she'll—"

"You can't cause then she'll know you was out here snoopin. Sit still."

He hits me just hard enough to sting but not loud enough for the noise to carry. I try to keep quiet so he won't know it hurts, but I just can't help myself. "You bastard," I call him again and again, my face pushed up hard against the spragnum moss.

"Hushup or I'll do it harder." He goes on hitting me. "You shoulda stayed," he says, and I dare say he almost sounds a little hurt. "You shoulda bin back thare bind the barn too but you waren't so now yer gittin what I got."

The air feels cool where he hit after he finishes. I stay like that for a minute letting the sting wear off and feeling spent and something else too—something like a tingle or a warmth. Then he moves a little and starts breathing fastly so I get up and push my nightgown back down and stand there in front of him trying not to cry.

"You should gwan home now," he says. "Reckon Abigail still wants them burries." He's still settin there under the tree, all hidden and covered in shadow. He plucks a handfulla berries from the bush and holds them out to me for the taking. I take them for now, but I still hate him even more than I did any of those other times when he ever played a trick on me or ratted me out to Rebecca. He pulled up my nightgown and now I'm standing here crying from the shame of it.

"You bastard," I say again. Then I turn and run real quick afore he can ketch me again.

I've stopped crying by the time I get back to Abigail's house. I climb slowly through the window and look at her tangled hair where it's all splayed out on the pillow, thinking about how much I'd like to grind the berries into it. But I also really wanna see them bones, so for now I lift the bottom of the bedspread and leave the huckleberries there in the gap between the bed and the floor. Then I run back across the moss, open the door so softly and crawl past Pa's room without even daring to breathe. I don't fall asleep right away. I lay there on my side with my hand tracing over the skin again and again where he hit me.

He lifted it and I being naked underneath and all, the bastard. I hate him and everything tingles and especially where he hit. I cried and somehow I'll get him. Somehow I'll—

And the sound of it, the noise around the barn, and how I sat there, listening.

He pulled up my nightgown and yet.

And yet.

Emma

He's wearing a sweater vest and writing in a little book, just like they always show them. There's that assumed wall of clinical compassion between us, but all I can think about is how I'm probably ruining his day.

"And are you able to enjoy things?" he asks.

"No, I feel guilty a lot. And these thoughts."

"What thoughts are those?"

"About dying. About—doing it."

"Thoughts about being killed? About something hurting you?"

"No, about—it's hard to say. About seeing myself—doing it—"

The pen scratches the pad decisively. "Is there a history of suicide in your family?" he asks.

See? You're fucking crazy.

"Not that I know of."

"Have you ever tried to kill yourself before?"

"No."

"But you find yourself thinking about it."

"Well, I can't tell what it is, if it's just anxiety, or if I actually want to—"

He lifts himself a little in his chair, settles back down again. "You really shouldn't try to differentiate it anyway. It's a problem you can't solve, no matter how hard you try."

"Yeah," I say, shaking.

He gets up and goes to sit in front of an old, yellowing computer. A light-bulb above us blinks, buzzes, fades slightly. For some time, the only sound I hear is the clicking mouse.

"Well," he says at last, "we usually start with Prozac."

"Ok."

"It will take a little time."

"Ok."

"There may be side-effects. You'll want to watch how much you drink. And for some people— well, how old are you?"

"Twenty-five."

"Ok, well, for some people under twenty-five, the risk of suicide actually goes up. If you experience that, or if you feel wound up or agitated, call us right away. And keep in mind it isn't you. It's the drug."

You know it isn't going to help you, right?

"Ok."

"And you say your mother recently passed away?"

"Yes."

"I'm sorry. I'm so sorry. Please call if you need to."

"Ok."

When I go to fill the prescription it's raining heavily—heavy drops falling from the heavy clouds on the heavy trees and running over the heavy stones. I walk across the street to the CVS, avoiding the aisles stocked with accessories and remedies meant for normal people: pain relievers, razor-blades, sleep aids. I take the innocuous white bag from the pharmacist's hand along with her "Give it a little time, hon." I go back outside where it's raining so heavily and walk down the stairs to get the train. When it approaches, the whole tunnel howls.

Go on –you could do it right now.

But I get on that train, holding tight to the strap as the car lurches jerkily along toward Davis Square, the sparks spurring us on along the track, so deep in that cold black tunnel in the earth, the car so heavy and groaning.

David

She had to go and ruin it. I only wanted to show her what she had coming but she had to go and ruin it. I wouldn't of even tried to get it if it hadn't been for her stealing that key. Then Joseph came down and she just had to drop it then—just had to, like maybe she even did it on purpose. Wouldn't put it past her neither. What else could I do then with her already gone and I had the apple palsy so bad I could barely stand up, so in the end it was just me settin down there alone by the barrel?

"I'll show you," he said and grabbed my shirt and pulled me up the stairs toward the barn. "I'll show you stealin and drinkin on the Lord's day. Youghta be ashamed."

And that wasn't even the worst part. The worst part was sneaking home afterward and Markie seeing me all sore and red-eyed.

So I sent Abigail to bring her to the bog. I kissed her and told her to go. I knew she'd do what I said if I kissed her.

But I was finished and she stayed there over my lap all naked there in the dark like she was waiting for me to keep on hitting her.

Why'd she have to ruin it? Why dint she just git up and run?

Rebecca

A great enterprise is what they're calling it. Mister Hawthorne and all them boys up there working for him from dawn to dusk, right out there on the bank of the Mullica. Aworking away on that mill when they should be down here minding their trades and families. So it follows for us stepping into their place and minding their counters and fields and mules and looking after their sons and daughters, all at the same time. So much gets left undone. A body can only do so much.

Look at Rachel for instance. You wouldn't even know what she is unless you really know her, though Lord knows I do what I can. I show her how to hold a needle and where to pull the thread, but you give it to her and she just sits there staring at it like she aint never seen one afore. But soon as you let her out the door she scoots straight off to the bog like she was born to it. And her mischief with Abigail, leading her to a bees' nest knowing full well how bad she'd swell up. I punished her right enough for it but it should've been her pa. But I did the duty in front of me and I pray something will come of it.

A great enterprise, they're calling it. As if we wasn't doing just fine afore.

Abigail

I did what he wanted with Rachel when he told me to get her to the bog somehow after dark when no one would know. He dint say why but I don't rightly care. Reckon I'll show her the bones tomorrow and it probly won't even matter in the end.

After I ask her to get the huckleberries I'm feeling pretty middling smart, so I decide to go help Rebecca with closing the store. I sweep up round the big bags of coffee beans and crocks-a cramberries and dust off the spice racks and wrap up what's left of the pies and make sure the guns are all stacked up neat in the corner by the plow and the saddles. I give Rebecca two pennies for a cake of soap and she throws in a bailey wax for my trouble. I smile at her when she does that, but truth is I'm thinking about David.

"You sweet little thing," she says. I like Rebecca cause she has no children so she watches over us all instead.

He kissed me and it wasn't even very short, right on my lips out there behind the garden where no one else could see. So I figure tomorrow after she's brung the berries I'll go ahead and show her where the bones are, and it won't even matter at all what he wanted with her out there in the cripple where no one could find them, the two of them all alone in the dark bog.

Emma

At home, on the sofa, under a blanket. Watching a couple episodes of *Futurama* and waiting to feel something. Sometimes I find myself crying and trying to put it all together, but each time something in my mind just sighs and makes a dismissive gesture, like it's fallen down and would rather stay on the ground. There's too much to know and I'm losing control and *Oh my God Oh my God what if I end up like her?*

Sometimes it feels like Mom is more here because she isn't. I sit there on the couch thinking about it, how the more you try to form your mind around a missing thing, the more of a shape it begins to take on until it seems like even your mind can't contain the thing that's missing, and how that missing thing begins to seem present in everything else; and then how everything effectively goes missing, since what those things once might have been in relation to the missing thing are now only inverted reflections of themselves. The book Mom used to read. The floor she used to walk. Everything slipping away. Goodbye, cruel world.

I'm thinking about that as I'm watching *Futurama* in the dim, cloudy light, not really watching since it's really all I can do to try and sleep just lying there, unmoving, unable to feel my bones.

Rachel

Soon as we're outside eating our lunches I find Abigail and ask her whether she got the huckleberries. She holds up her hand so I can see her fingernails are stained from the juice. It makes me wanna hit her a little bit.

"How'd you git past Miss Mullin this marnin?"

"Sometimes she skips me. Says she don't need to look." She smiles that smile that makes me remember why I don't like her sometimes. "Thank you for the burries," she says, smiling. I really wanna hit her but Miss Mullin's standing nearby watching over us all, so I can't. I do poke her hard on the shoulder though.

"Today after school," I tell her, and each word's got a poke to go with it. "Meet me bind the barn or I'll tell Miss Mullin bout yer hands."

The smile goes away at that.

Afterward we all go inside to do our sums and then we hear something about the Decoration of Independence and how they used to make cannonballs outta bog iron for the continental army right down the river in Atsion, and on and on and on all the way up to Mister Lincoln and the Mancipation Proclamation. By then I'm sore from settin and itching to go outside again. I'm the first one out when Miss Turner rings her bell. David sits toward the back cause he's older but I don't wait for him this time. I just go straight out and run down the dusty road so I can get to the path behind the barn afore Rebecca can find me to help in the store. I been waiting there probly about five minutes when Abigail finally comes creeping round the wall. I can tell she's afeared already cause of the way she keeps looking around behind her, like she's trying to find someone who can help her.

"You member whare it is?"

She nods, unspeaking.

"Alright, let's go. And no runnin way neither. Member what I told you."

Abigail likes to pretend she knows the woods but truth is she hardly ever goes there. She can't stand the skeeters and the green-heads and the little floating clouds of no-see-ums. I can tell from the way she's walking down the path and always looking to the side like she's got it in her head to find a snake or a spider curled up there. Once I yell out *Snake!* just for the fun of it and she almost runs away screaming. She's always acting like she knows the way of things but underneath it all she's just afeared.

We come up over the crest-a the hill by Tom's Folly, and I know we're getting close cause Abigail is walking a little faster than she was earlier, like she wants to get it over with. She leads us down and diagonal across the little hill and we go slow and gangly-like through the bushes and the devil grass. Soon we come to a patch of jailhouse oaks that are tall and straight and thick, with a little pool of water inside. The thickest trunk is all hollowed out. Abigail points to it and we go over and crouch down inside the cell of the trees, right in front of the dark maw.

She points. "In thare. Lookit."

Sure enough I can see something crouching back there in the shadow underneath the overhanging trunk: a tiny grey thing half-submerged in the water, no biggern a baby's hand. Mosquito worms are spasming around it and I reckon they'll be just about growed up soon. I look and look at it, trying to find the skull, some teeth, a spine.

"How you think it died?" she asks.

"Musta got stuck in thare. When they're that little they gotta hard enough time seein as it is."

"You know what it is?"

"Probly a baby rabbit, bein that small."

"What happened to it?"

"Probly started stormin and rainin one day and it couldn't git out. And the ma probly got the others out and this one was the runt and she couldn't go back to git it with lookin after the others an all."

"Why dint it just run away?" Abigail says.

"Probly dint know any better. Probly drowned an choked in the wooder an when it died all its skin fell off an a passel-a maggots came an ate all its guts out."

For a minute Abigail looks like she might just spew her breakfast all over them tree trunks.

"Well I done showed it to you just like I said I would," she says after a minute. "Let's go now."

I sit there staring and staring at that footy little thing under the tree, just trying the whole time not to laugh. Truth is I'm not at all convinced it's even dead. Might as well be a pebble or a root or a little Indian bread for all the good it's doing down there. But Abigail's such a goody-goody all the time—serves her right to be even more afeared now and then.

"Rachel!"

"I'm comin."

Joseph

They say a month till it's done but I suspect less. Figure they'll be cutting that ribbon in three weeks or so, way they're out there working most nights.

Suppose we'll have to widen the road for the jags going out. The ladies won't approve of that so much for their gardens but reckon they'll just have to put themselves aside for the good of the town like the rest of us. It'll be a sight for sure, though, seeing them all go back into their houses just like that after holding down the trades for so long. Just so all them business types up in Trenton and New York can wrap up their passels in a good piece-a Cedar Furnace stock. Imagine Mister Hawthorne'll get a few angry letters for that one.

They'll be cutting it in three weeks and it'll be something to see, that's for sure. The mill all shiny-red and new-painted and the jack already broke into and spoiled. Damn shame, though I have to say it was a pretty good stunt. Couldn'ta done it better myself. Hardly a drop spilled on the ground so I almost got to feeling bad giving him that rat-tanning. But I don't want folks saying I'm getting too old to teach a good lesson.

Odd thing that he went and broke into the cellar, though, who's never done anything like it afore. One of the other boys must've put him up to it. At any rate a boy that age'll be hard at work pulping soon enough stead of going round breaking into folks' homes. Good thing in the end, I suppose. Only thing a town needs morn a church is a place for its sons to go to work. Or so Mister Hawthorne tells us, up there in that big house of his.

It's a little after noon now so I go ahead and walk on down the road to the stable to feed Abe. He watches me outta the side of his head as he eats, his jaw just going and going in his skull.

"Thare you go now, Abe," I say, patting his bony-ridged face. "Thare you go now, old boy."

Rebecca

I'm wrapping up the coffee grinder for Missus Hawthorne when they come arunnin in, a jumble-a sun-darkened limbs in muslin dresses, all covered up in muck just like I figured they would be. But earlier than I expected, nonetheless.

"Afternoon, girls."

"Afternoon, mam," says Abigail.

Rachel is standing there in the doorway too, trying not to laugh and looking down at her worn old shoes. I dare say I remember that gesture.

"Go an wash yarselves up so you look half-decent when you take this grinder on over to Missus Hawthorne. Then, Abigail, I'll need you to help me with the tailorin. Rachel, see if you can't find Joshua to bring a bagga meal on over from the mill. Make sure you have him tie it good an tight this time. I don't want it goin to waste all over my floor again."

"Yesmam," says Abigail.

"Now go an wash yarselves up."

"Yesmam," says Abigail.

Afore long they're out there laughing and splashing by the well. You wouldn't know it hearing them that when they're not here minding me they're usually snag-gagging and bullyragging. Normally I'd take the grinder myself but I'm hoping it'll put them on good behavior to see to a businessman's wife.

Late afternoon now. I look out the window but there's only the dust rising up off the road.

I think I missed him today. I musta missed

him today.

Abigail

We're walking on over to Mister Hawthorne's house when Rachel says she's got half a mind to go on back to the woods, stead of going on to the mill like Rebecca said. I tell her I'll rat her out if she does and that keeps her quiet for awhile.

As we're walking down the road toward the big house I'm thinking about the huckleberries. I wanna ask Rachel what happened over there in the cripple, but she aint been too forthcoming about any of that so I decide to hush about it. Anyway a lady shouldn't ask after what it's not her business to know.

But whatever it was I hope it was worth them berries. It couldn'ta been too bad after all that she's already talking about going back. And who can fault me for wanting to know what he wanted with her out there in the dark, the two of them out there all alone.

We keep on walking down the road.

"Did you have any trouble gittinum?" I ask.

"Gittin what."

"The burries."

"No."

And that's all she says.

But if she aint lying what else could he have wanted with her out there in the bog?

But a lady shouldn't go asking after others' business, so I hush about it for now.

Soon we come to the gate in the white fence around Mister Hawthorne's house and head on up along the worn path to the door. They painted it dark red and there's a bright white gable round the door and all the windows. Pa says it's to show they got lashins o money and that's why they got a passel-a people working forum out there on the river.

Rachel's carrying the grinder so I go ahead and reach up and hammer the iron knocker. We stand out there in the sun with the cicadas humming on and on in the trees till Millie Hawthorne comes and opens the door and smiles down at us.

"Just look at you two ladies," she says. "All grown up and out on business!"

Her dress is deep red and kinda wrinkled, and the way she smells is making Rachel sneeze. Her skin so white and pale you can almost see the veins underneath—I dare say even Rachel might be prettiern her. Looking at her now I get to wondering if it's true what my pa told my ma about their daughter up and dying, and it puts a right chill deep in my bones. But I also sorta like to visit Missus Hawthorne cause if you look real hard through the door you can just see the wallpaper there inside the parlor and the crystal chandelier they brung in all the way from Philadelphia. Reckon if I do all the deliveries from now on maybe she'll even let me wear a little of her perfume next time I wanna find David.

She hands us the money for the grinder and we say good day and thank you. Then we climb down the steps from the porch and head back toward the road. And Rachel keeping so quiet the entire time you wouldn't even know she was there.

"I really did like them burries," I say.

"Well I'm glad," she says, though she don't really sound it.

"It waren't hard gittinum?"

"Nope."

By the time we get over the bridge I'm sure she's lying. She aint been looking at me at all.

"Rachel Morris, you tell me what happened out thare this minute."

"What you mean what happened."

"I know somethin happened out thare in the woods and that's why yaint talkin."

"Nethin happened in the woods. I just got the burries like yasked."

"Then why won't you talk about it?"

She's dragging her foot through the sand on the bridge. "Aint nethin to talk about! Why you carr about it anyways?"

"Just things happen in the woods at night is all."

"Yer just scard."

"I beant scard. I just know sometimes things happen in the woods at night when it's dark and the devil's out runnin."

"Revernd Samuel tell you that?"

"No. I just know is all."

"Well nethin happened and thare waren't no devil. I got the burries an brungum back is all."

"Yer a lyin little sneak. I'll find yout soon enough an tell Rebecca what you bin up to."

"Just you try. You won't find nethin. I told you. I got the burries an brungum back is all. Leave me alone."

And she goes on walking ahead down the road toward the stable, without waiting for me, without so much as even turning around.

Millie

So much light and life in those girls. Especially the ragged one—I dare say she would have liked my Cathy.

More light, he says. More roses! Windows! Windows!

Rail on, you old bastard—a fly throws itself against a window pane, insisting what's transparent isn't there. I know better. I've learned to forget about the things of this world.

Each night she comes to me in glory, blinding in her radiance. She comes to call me home, a bird back to the nest.

I am the light of the world. Whoever follows me will never walk in darkness, but will have the light of life.

Every night, I'm less and less afraid.

Emma

Barely slept. Thoughts of needles and knives appearing out of nowhere. A popping balloon under my ribs: Ba-BUM. Ba-BUM. Ba-BUM.

At work everyone is asking what we have on the Higgs particle. I probably pull the same book three or four times. When they ask me what I think about it, my mind turns inward and gets stuck there. Seems a waste to be thinking about the future and its physics when getting through a day is hard enough. And I probably won't even live to see the future anyway—

Catastrophic thinking. Should remember to tell Karen.

They said to give it a couple weeks, and it's been a couple weeks. Must be a really bad case.

Probably doomed from the start. Maybe I'll even start cutting myself and then I'll have to live with the scars for the rest of my life, which probably won't even be very long because I'll probably—

Just do it you fucking coward.

Never thought it would be like this. Not what they promised. Not what we worked for. Blame the economy, they say.

But who do I blame for Mom? For this?

Some people have real problems. Cancer. Starvation. War.

This isn't supposed to be happening to me.

Entitled, much? Go fuck yourself.

Karen says it's a waste of energy to dwell on the negative. Letting it go. Letting it go.

Co-workers are all engaged in a very serious and anxious discussion about why they aren't hipsters. Seems like the easiest thing to do to prove you aren't a hipster is to come out and say that you are—and to mean it, too, earnestly and un-ironically—since a real hipster probably couldn't do it. He'd already know better, already know everything.

I don't know a single thing anymore.

Me, me, me. I, I, I. Pathetic.

Embrace the moment, she says.

Run the credit card through. Thank you. Have a nice day.

Rachel

After we make the delivery I decide to stop in the woods afore going on to ask Joshua for the flour. Abigail says she'll tell so I hit her and that keeps her quiet for awhile. Serves her right for asking so many questions anyway.

The air is always colder in the cripple with the cedars and it's always a little darker. They say the sea used to cover this place and sometimes I think about fish swimming up around the trees. I even like to think I'll find a ghost dancing around in there one day like old Joe Mulliner. But reckon today I'll settle for finding a snakeskin for leaving under Abigail's blanket.

I also wanna get some more berries and have some to take back for Pa afore he comes home. I aint been back since going to find the bones, and I'm still feeling a little outta sorts about the other night. But there's no reason why he woulda followed me from Mister Hawthorn's place. I don't even have the key to Joseph's cellar no more since I left it in the drawer beneath the counter in the store, so Rebecca won't know I ever took it.

So I tell myself it's silly and go up through the trees to where the berries are and I sit there under the bush eating them and listening to the chickadees and blue jays and whippoorwills squabbling up around the pine cones. I know if I sit quiet enough a deer might pass by to pick at the berries and I can try to feed it from my hand, though it only worked once with a fawn. Other times I might jump out from behind a bush to scare them so they rear up and run away, tearing up the leaves and the needles with their eyes rolling back white in their skulls. But they always come back for the berries.

I been settin there awhile waiting when I hear something coming up the hill. I crouch down behind the bush expecting it to be a deer or Rebecca. But it's David, and his eyes are darting round like he's looking for something.

I'm still a little mad at him from afore, so I reach out and grab a fistful-a berries from the bush and throw them right at him.

He lets out a cuss when they hit him and spatter on his shirt. Then he looks up at the bush and sees me. "*You*," he says through his teeth and makes toward me.

But I know what to do and where the crik runs, so I take off from the bushes and run deeper into the bog to the edge of the little stream where the trees stand up stark and straight and bone-white against the sky. Afore he can ketch me I'm already in the water yards out from the bank, and all he can do is stand there watching me. He picks up a stone and throws it toward me but it goes off wide and sets an old eph screeching and flapping up out of the shallows. He don't know how to swim so I know I'm safe for now.

"Yer gon git it for gittin yer dress wet," he yells.

"Go way. I aint talkin to you."

"Yer talkin to me right now!"

"I beant." I duck my head under so I can't hear what he says next. I'm really just hoping he'll go away. But when I come back up he's still there pacing.

"You know you desarved it, right?" he's yelling from the bank. "You know I was just givin you what yalready had comin?"

"Aint up to you," I say and stick my tongue out at him from the water.

But to tell you the truth, as mad as I want it to sound, I dare say something is waking up there in the crik. I suddenly feel like showing off a little so I stretch out and float on the surface belly-up.

"Damn right it is," he says. "You woulda got away with it too. It aint right." He watches me all stretched out there in the wooder and his expression softens a little all of a sudden. "Oh, what the hell. Come on back in an I'll git you a blanket."

"How I know you won't hit me again."

"You know I won't. Come on back in, Rachel."

He suddenly looks so unhappy there standing on the bank with his purple-stained shirt that I decide I've paid him back enough and start swimming back toward the bank. When I climb up on the shore he backs away a little as if he's afeared to touch me. We walk on back toward the stable, slow and unspeaking, and when we get there he pulls down one of the horse blankets from the loft and hands it to me. It has little bits of straw in it and smells like the mules when I wrap myself up, but soon I'm feeling warmer standing there by the empty stalls, and David looking so worked up in his purply shirt that pretty soon I actually get to feeling a little bit bad about things.

"I dint mean to git it on yer shirt," I say, even though it's a lie. "And I dint mean for us to git caught." That last bit is true.

"I know. I was just mad is all. Dint seem right you waren't thare."

I'm not about to tell him how I was there, listening so close from the edge of the cripple, so I say, "Warn't right for you to send Abigail neither. Now she won't stop askin me about it."

He turns and looks at me for a long time. "If yer so worried," he says, "why dint you just run?"

I suppose maybe I could tell him about the tingling I got out there settin by the stable while I listened, and that night in the bog and in bed afterward and in the water this morning. But then afore I know it something starts kicking up again right there in the stable, and suddenly I can't look at him and it don't seem right but then again it don't seem altogether wrong neither, and I'm standing there feeling the warmth spreading and spreading and wondering if this aint a sin like the kind Reverend Samuel's always going on about.

"I dunno," I say.

I keep standing there for a little while cause I'm not sure what else to do, just listening to the mules nickering and pawing the dirt in the pasture.

And soon enough I think I hear someone else coming. I look out and see it's Joseph walking on down the road in that slow way of his. I look around to warn David but it appears he's heard it too and he's already gone. Then I think I might also hear Rebecca calling, so I go on right away out the stable around through the back so no one will see, and what with David asking about that other night and with Joseph coming on down the road, truth is I never been more relieved to hear Rebecca calling me to come back to the store. Even though I never even got the flour that she asked for.

Emma

Kate calls me after work.

"Jesus, Emma! I've been calling and calling. What the hell—"

"Nothing. I just have a favor to ask. I want to know about Mom."

"—what? What about her?"

"I want to know about her. You know. What her life was like. I just want to know."

"Uh, listen, Emma—"

"Can you send me the photos from the shoebox?"

"Emma, listen. Do you want me to come up there? Cause I can, if you want. I can jump in the car and drive up there tonight."

"No, I'm fine. Really. But can you send me the photos? Can you just do that?"

"I mean, yeah, sure. It'll be a few days, though—I have to get them from Dad. Why do you want them?"

Because they might just make me feel something.

"I don't really know. I just need them."

Hawthorne

All is moving according to schedule, with minimal accident. A mere fall and a broken arm thus far, nothing unexpected. Truly the Lord is good and sees to His own. So Isaiah once told us, and John after him: *I am the voice of one calling in the wilderness, 'Make straight the way of the Lord'.* And so even we who have suffered must endeavor.

I imagine no more than a fortnight now. It will be precisely what this little hamlet needs, ever since the furnace went idle and its men along with it. The truth is that they're perfectly willing to work, so long as there's work to be had. All it needs is a guiding hand.

Everyone has enough iron these days, it seems, ever since the rush in Pennsylvania. But paper will be something different. The old Cedar Furnace, soon to be the Cedar Paper Mill, and a good thing, too. It certainly wouldn't do to keep on with the old way: everyone simply walking their fields and seeing to their mules and their trades, simply living and dying on the same piece of land without ever knowing what it's worth. But to have some real industry again, real shipments going out and real profits coming in—that will be something this town has never seen before. A good roll of packing paper will get you more these days than a few iron pots ever could. It will give them a reason to rejoice, to give thanks.

This house, too. Perfectly good, for an iron-master. Now it simply needs a little attention, a patient hand to guide it back into its time. Millie fought me on the chandelier, but I suspect more light will do her good with her condition. Perhaps we might even have a couple windows added in the parlor and the library. And the little garden is to be expanded, tilled and planted with beets, corn, and peanuts, so that those not working in the mill or out logging and harvesting the grass will not remain idle. There will be plenty of honest work for honest men who want it, and the mill to make a place on the map for this town. At last, one might take a little pride being born and raised here in Cedar Mill.

Yes, indeed, I believe we can make another start here. We'll make a true gentleman's farm out of it, soon enough.

Rebecca

Looks like I missed him today. I been watching the road but I musta missed him today.

Perhaps to send Rachel just to see that everything is well. She'll be coming back from the gristmill soon enough.

Yes—maybe just to send her on down the road. Just to make sure all is well.

David

I run outta the stable when I see Joseph coming and crouch down there in the woods while he leads that old horse of his in, a bagga bones ugly and long-legged as he is.

And I see Rachel slipping out around the back just in time too. She goes arunnin down the road toward the store, something about her so damned determined and quick, her wet hair hanging long and dark and dripping down her back, leaving a little muddy trail in the dust behind her. She done left that blanket in the stable. Her dress is wet and clinging so close around her, her thin legs beneath a wild blur.

I keep watching till I know she's away and safe. Then I make my way back deeper into the woods, along through the bog and toward the crik where she jumped in afore, where the mud's been stirred up so bad the water looks sorta like a dish fulla milky tea. Pretty soon I come across a couple-a sundews at water's edge, growing up from a mounda sugar sand, all sticky-sweet and sap-beaded. And in one of them I can just make out a little black antmire struggling in the filaments, the tendril just beginning to curl close around it, just starting to whisper of honey and sleep.

I can hearum pounding away under the sun. Out there across the stream and further up along the river and down along past the very edge of the cedars and the cramberry bog, right overtop them big canals they all dug. Just working and working away on that mill as if there's no tomorrow.

Morris

When you're out there working under the sun, something happens you don't rightly reckon on: you forget how many hours there are in a day. Seems instead like you spend all your time just setting out there in the heat with hardly any rain for days and days, watching as the walls up and build themselves around you.

Which aint to say we beant working the skin off our backs getting Mister Hawthorn's mill up and runnin, scraping and sawing and pounding it together day after day, toiling like a passel-a antmires from sunup to sundown. It wears on a body pretty hard, but I dare say there's something fitting about building it outta the same stuff that'll go right into the product. Well, the bark of it anyway. Whole lotta devil grass too, I suppose. Either way it gets into you somehow. Even after washing up you can smell the sweet breath of it at night.

Sarah would've been behind it. Not like so many of the ladies in town these days who go round murmuring and snag-gagging as if to rouse the dead. Sarah would've liked it, sure enough. I try to remember that's really why we're out here in the end. It aint the butcher's paper or the profit calls us out to the river, but the land and the families all needing tending.

I ketch myself thinking about Rachel all the time. She runs around and it aint right. I know it aint right. But truth is I'm hoping it'll make things a little better, my being out here and her without her ma from the very beginning. She oughta have a new set of clothes fit for extra meetins and a nice upheader to bring her there and back. Reckon she don't know it yet, but I see the way the boys are all watching her grow up tall and strong and her eyes bright and green and her hair dark and curly. So I figure it'll be worth it in the end, having the mill to rely on for the younger ones and seeing them settle down in the same town that succored them.

Sure, reckon it won't be so bad in the end that we spent these last couple-a months sweating and toiling out here on the Mullica, doing good by our town and our children.

Emma

I'm looking down at the box that contains my mother's life. My arms stretch long with the weight of her as I carry her into the house. Carefully, I put her down on the kitchen table. The cardboard lid is flabby. When I lift it there's a whiff of damp air. She used to keep them under the staircase in the basement, piled up in the box and wrapped in a plastic grocery bag.

A couple of them are already face-up and familiar. Mom standing in the driveway in her first communion dress. Mom with Nanna sitting on the front porch steps of the new house in Waldwick. Mom with Dad sitting next to a sleeping infant Kate, laughing and pointing at her pudgy arm draped over an empty beer bottle.

There's no order to them whatsoever, and even now this seems strange coming from her. Mom was always so careful to document our lives, kept books full of photos under her bedroom table arranged according to date and name and occasion. It used to amaze us how she could recall each day and event and location involving her children simply from the photographic tilt in a slant of sunlight. This, while the evidence of her own life—of everything that had led up to those later moments—remained hidden away in the box.

I don't really know what else to do, so I start taking them out one by one and laying them out on the table. The old, faded ones I put to the left: mostly of my mother's pale child's face peering out from a background of shadows bled through with sepia sunlight, nearly unrecognizable except for the odd eyebrow or nose from which we'd later spring, miraculously, as if born right out of her skull. From there I start working up, laying them down by date, by photo quality, by any perceived narrative I can summon. I spend the whole afternoon like that, just laying photos out on the table while the rain keeps plummeting outside the window, each drop a little bomb coming heavily down, rolling lethargically down along off the leaves and so slowly bursting on the sidewalk.

Joseph

She gives me a start when she runs into the stable, limbs and hair all akimbo, panting and soaked to the skin and smelling like mud and sap and wildness.

She immediately goes off saying something about how Rebecca sent her afore I can even open my mouth to ask her what she wants. So it's all I can do to tell her yes, everything's fine—that she can go ahead and let Rebecca know it's fine—that she only missed me walking down the road for tending to the store and the customers that needed tending to. And I dare say that as she scoots out she scowls after me, going on down the road toward the mill instead of straight back to the store like she oughta. It puts me in the mind to remember Rebecca all those years ago, with her whip-smart little smirk.

I let Abe back out to pasture and watch him going out, carrying that worn-out sack of a body back into the sunshine—a good for nothing durgen, scarred as hell, just hanging on like some old machine that won't die. Though you'd never think he knew it, way he's lipping at the mares across the way. You'd never think there's that side to him, something remaining that remembers its youth, as if time aint the thing in actuality but the mere idea of the thing washing up like a wave outta the sea and tumbling you and finally going on, leaving you alive and, if you're lucky, understood by someone. Broken, sure. But alive, and understood, and a little of the old badness still in you.

Abigail

After Rebecca sends us home from the store and I gone and et my supper with Ma and Pa, I sit there by my window looking out at the woods, watching the growing dark bloom up in the east and the trees turning thick and black against it like dark veins.

I'm looking over at Rachel's house thinking about her out there in the woods alone with David.

And it gets me thinking about the kinda things no lady should ever think about. Pretty soon I tell myself to stop it. And I do, for a time.

But as I'm lying there trying to sleep the thoughts keep coming back. It seems the more I think about not thinking about them the more I think about them anyway. Soon they get to really worrying me and I even start praying to stay safe and pure. But the thoughts just keep coming and coming.

I look back out through the window to Rachel's house, just to see if her little red candle is lit. But it's dark over there and silent as a grave, if not for the peepers cooing out in the bog.

I try to get to sleep again.

But then so soon I see them again in my mind, and suddenly they aren't wearing clothes and he's doing more than kissing her like he kissed me and I can't bear it. I just can't bear it.

Afore I know it I'm up outta bed and crawling out through the window in my nightgown. I'm runnin across the way toward the side of the house where her window peers out and where the candle sits now, unlit and lonesome there in the dark. I stand there under the window listening. At first I don't think I hear anything, so I suppose it's safe looking up over the sill. But it's too dark in there to see anything, and meantime I'm starting to get kinda nervous. I try calling after her in a whisper.

"Rachel."

I hear her rustling under the blanket and she makes a little groan in her sleep. Then I hear her settin up. Her voice floats down low and groggy and annoyed over the sill.

"What."

"It's me."

"Who's me," she snaps.

"You know who. Listen. I aint leavin till you tell me so you better tell it straight what happened out thare in the woods."

"What you mean in the woods."

"With the burries."

"Damn it, Abigail! Dint I tell you afore it waren't nethin?"

"He dint kiss you or nethin?"

"Gollykeeser no!"

I dare say she sounds pretty earnest. But I have to be sure anyway. "You sware it on yer Ma's grave?"

Her voice goes low and hissy. "I sware!" Reckon she's really mad now since I gone and mentioned her ma.

"Alright. But you better not be lyin. I'll know it if yare. David'll tell me if yer lyin."

"Reckon he won't," she says in the middle of a yawn, the pick she's got on me already dying. "Gwan back to sleep and leave me alone afore I hafta wake Pa up and tell him how much of a nuisance yer bein."

But I don't go yet. She's gone and rubbed me the wrong way calling me a nuisance and talking about David like that.

"He would too tell me!" I whisper-shout back. "He would too cause you know what he did? He kissed me out thare bind Mister Hawthorne's garden. So thare. What you think of that?"

"Reckon he dint!"

"He did an right on my lips too. Right afore he sent me on to git you. An I think he likes me morn you and someday we're gon get doubled up an have ourselves a baby. What you think of that now?"

"Reckon you'll make him a rotten wife and yer kids'll all be ugly."

Something about the way she says it is awful, not the words in themselves but the actual sound of the words, like it weren't even hard for her to say, like it's something she knows deep down that I don't.

"Gwan with you!"

"Well you asked an that's what I think. I was jist being honest," she says. "Leave me alone now, wouldya? We got church in the marnin."

"Alright. Fine. But you jist think about that. You jist magine him kissin me an see if you kin sleep some."

At that I run back across to my window. After I've crawled back in and gotten under the blanket I sit there looking back toward the house and the sill. The little red candle is still out. All the housen are silent and there's only the noise of the peepers and the crickets coming on down along the trees from the bog. And Ma and Pa snoring like a bellows through the daubin, there in the room next to mine.

Emma

There she is. No more than twenty, a slender girl with bobbed hair in a cotton floral dress, sitting on another woman's lap in the front seat of a Ford Model N.

On the back of it, a note written out in a flowing, fountain-pen hand, faded and partially scribbled out: ________ *Molly Lowell, Mount Laurel, NJ. August 2nd, 1906.*

I know from the smile and the freckle on her

temple that it's Nanna sitting there in the front seat of the car. I can't say who the other one is. Her face is covered, her arms alone visible where they're wrapped tight around my grandmother's waist.

I never thought to ask Mom about it back when I was younger, when the purview of what could comfortably be called 'family' often stopped with my grandmother. Family back then simply was what it was. The why of it hadn't begun to matter.

But maybe Kate will know. Kate might at least have thought to ask.

It's getting dark and I haven't left the kitchen since bringing the photos in. I think about taking a shower and head into the bathroom to pee. I stay there sitting on the toilet long after I'm done peeing, just looking at the razor up there on the shower caddy, something in my chest tightening up so that it suddenly looks a little blurry sitting there.

It's just a thought.

I step into the shower and turn on the water and go ahead and shave my legs slowly and carefully.

It's only a thought.

I put the razor back up in the caddy and climb out of the shower, cold and dripping. I dry off quickly, throw on an oversized t-shirt and go to bed like that, my hair all wet and tangled on the pillow since I didn't bother with conditioner.

The air outside is humid and cold and couched in mist.

Rachel

I never thought she'd do it, crossing all the way over to my room after dark. I really dint think she'd ever do it. Reckon something put her up to it. Something bold and strong, or maybe just stupid.

That's what I'm thinking about settin in church this morning right in the pew next to Pa while Reverend Samuel stands up there on the pulpit going on and on about the Prodigal Son, his long, gray jowls quaking and quivering with rage. Looking back along the wall, I can just see David settin there in his usual place with his folks, between his Ma and Pa and his little brother Markie, looking alright in his white cotton shirt and his hair slicked back smooth and dark. I still aint talked to him since that time in the stable but I know it for a fact that he thinks the jowls are funny too, so I turn around and watch him just until I know I ketched his eye. Once I know he's seen me I pull down a little on the skin on both sides of my chin so it looks to be hanging down loose, and I let my bottom lip go too, so that my bottom teeth are showing just over my lip, and even though he looks away I think I probly see him smile. Then Pa sees what I'm doing and pinches me, so I turn back around in the pew.

Pretty soon Reverend Samuel starts asking for the collection to help feed our poor brothern and sistern living out there alone in the woods and to help get the mill built over on the Mullica so we can all live to see God's kingdom realized here on Earth, since it's true and right that we do this and since the Scriptures say in no uncertain terms that we oughta love our neighbors same as ourselves. I look up at the anxious seat where Abigail usually sets with her Ma and Pa and her little sister Molly there on both sides of her. She's nodding and nodding in her fancy ruffled dress, right in front of the pulpit.

After the service we all go outside to stand and talk and drink lemonade and eat the cookies Rebecca brung. I'm biting the head off a gingerbread man when I see David coming out with his Ma, and she standing there and talking on and on with Rebecca while David just waits there looking more bored than I ever seen him afore, just dragging his foot in the sand and sighing. Then I see Abigail walk over and tell him good day and twirl a little in her dress like she wore it just for him. And David looking more bored than I think I ever seen him look afore.

By ten o'clock we're all starting on back to our homes to honor the Lord's day with rest and contemplation. Pa turns to me and pushes a little of my hair behind my ear, so I know he's ready to leave. He tells me that he's gonna bring a coupla pickerel home for supper and that I oughta go on and spend some time with Abigail and the girls while he's out there fishing and smoking on the river. I dare say I see him looking over at David for a minute when he says that, so I say alright and he kisses the top of my head and tips his hat to Rebecca and Missus Cranmer and he shakes Reverend Samuel's hand and goes on walking down the road. Missus Cranmer goes on talking with Rebecca, the two of them looking over towards me as I wave. Then they just keep on talking. David's looking so bored now that even Abigail's given up on getting him to say something. I'm getting bored standing there too, so I leave them there and walk on away from the church a little over toward the graveyard, where Pa says his ma was buried and her ma even afore that and where Ma's bones are resting now too.

Walking and weaving through the headstones,

I get back to thinking about what Abigail said outside the window last night in the dark. I wonder for a minute if it's true that he kissed her. But when I try to see it in my mind—how they woulda looked standing there kissing—I just start giggling to myself. It seems so wrong somehow that anyone would ever wanna kiss Abigail. She's so much shorter than all the others and David already taller than I am. He musta bent halfway over to kiss her.

"What you laughin at?"

When I look up he's standing there with his hair still slicked back and parted down the middle. I dare say he looks kinda handsome all fancied up like that.

"Nethin."

I guess I musta looked a little startled when he appeared. He's laughing at me. "Shoulda seen yer face," he says. "Who'd you think I was, that Hawthorne girl comin to hauntya?"

"Aw, hushup—you know that aint nethin but a loada hogwash."

"Yeah? Bet if I was to tellya I just saw'r ghost walkin out thare in the woods you'd believe me."

"Well didja?"

"Naw."

"Hushup then. My pa says it aint true an he never lies."

He shrugs. "Reckon it don't matter none anyway. She's probly off hauntin some sewer over in Phila—"

"Hushup, dammit! She waren't much oldern us!"

He looks a little shocked at that, puts up his hands with his palms toward me. "Alright. Alright.

Dint mean no harm by it."

After that we just watch each other for a little while as the sun warms the top of our heads. He pulls up a waving piece-a devil grass and sticks it in his mouth

"What you doin over thare anyways?" he says, sucking at the stem all thoughtful.

"Not much, I spose."

I start climbing up on top one-a the stones with my two arms out to balance just for the heck of it. He frowns a little seeing me do that, the grass drooping.

"Aw, Rachel, you shouldn't. It aint respecful. Come on down from thare now."

But I reckon these old dead folks already know everything. They probly aint too concerned with what goes on over their graves here on earth, so I keep on walking along the stone and balancing there over the grave of some old gentleman named Nathaniel Carson, who ainta any relation to anyone still living in the town far as I know.

"Come on down, Rachel," he says again, looking like something's started to hurt him.

"Bet you can't make me. Bet yer too scard to even come over near the grave."

"I beant scard."

"Bet yare though. Yer scarda bony old Mister Carson reachin right up through the ground an grabbin yer shoe. I bet you won't even come over to the stone."

"I'll come over to the stone right enough."

"Well I aint movin till you do. Reckon Mister Carson don't mine too much up thare in heaven. Or down in hell. Either way, reckon he don't mine."

"Yer pa'd stirrup you good to hear you talkin like that. Git on down like I said afore I go git him."

But I decide to stay there balancing, and David looking more and more uncomfortable over there by the edge of the graveyard—a little shocked even soon as I decide to start jumping up and down right on the top of that headstone.

"Aint up to you. But I guess I'll do it if you come on over to the stone."

I made him mad often enough to recognize the way his hands ball up into little white-knuckled fists, even while the look on his face don't change. He don't normally like to show off a pick when he's got one, but I can always see it.

"I sware it, Rachel," he says, sending a little something through me I can't rightly see. "I sware I'll do it."

"Come on over to the stone then."

He's just watching me standing there on the stone, and I can't say he looks all that shocked anymore. I dare say something about him gets determined after a little while, settling there in his jaw. He starts weaving in and out between the stones and making toward me with his hands all tight and balled up the way they get, and suddenly I'm losing my nerve and climbing down off the stone afore he even gets to where I'm standing. I'm arunnin so fast along to the edge of the graveyard, all the way up to where it's bordered by the woods, and afore I even know what I done or where I'm going I'm leaping that fence, feeling all warm again of a sudden, just runnin there through the woods and weaving in and out between the bull pines, him gaining on me the whole time judging from his footfalls on the needles and the loam. And soon I'm runnin outta breath and starting to wonder what he'll do when he ketches me—the two of us just runnin and runnin and feeling so warm all of a sudden out there in the woods, leading each other away from all our familiar places.

Rebecca

After church I think about trying to get out to the woods. The walk is long but it's been some time. I figure the store'll keep just fine till Monday—not to mention a long walk might just do me some good.

I take my leave of the ladies and the Reverend and start heading down the road toward the stable and the woods. On the way I look out toward the pasture—since Joseph didn't come to hear the sermon—but it's only the mules out there walking and eating and swinging their tails against the green heads. There's a quietness in the air I aint heard since the mill got started and it's really quite pleasant.

When I get to the little path that goes in toward the cripple behind the stable, I see it's gotten wider some. I think about Rachel ducking back here and I'm hoping I don't run into her walking through the cedars. Way she is she'll get to wondering what it is I'm doing out here, and then she won't ask so much as come out looking to see the thing I'm doing. So I'm hoping that maybe she went on to the river with her Pa for the day and they'll be out there fishing till dusk.

I walk on through the damp, cool shadows. It feels like the breeze is just pushing me onward, breathing and exhaling through the cedars and the brush. All around me the trees are creaking from it—

It's her, It's her—but I don't like to think about that too much, so I just keep on walking along through the cripple and dodging the little pool holes and huckleberry bushes and clumps of neverwet, the vines hanging down loose and entrail-like and bodily from the trees all around.

Soon I come to the little crik that runs down from the Mullica. I cross it on an overturned log that someone musta let down for a bridge. Just after that there's a point with one fork going on narrow and sparse and overgrowed into a patch of mountain laurel. To anyone else it might look like a dead end.

But it's just past that—I know, it's just past that—where the little clearing starts to open up.

And he's right there on the edge of it, waiting for me.

Abigail

I never been so tired in all my life.

I know it's shameful but it's the Lord's honest truth that I never been so tired in my life. And it was only cause Molly was there to pinch me that I dint start nodding off and snoring right there in that pew. Tonight I gotta get to sleep somehow. I gotta keep my mind clean and try to get to sleep.

But truth is I'm still a little worried about David, and now he won't even give me the time of day. I'm looking around for Rachel after he's gone and not seeing either one-a them there in the churchyard and not knowing where they both coulda gone off to. I try to think maybe they went to different places. I try to tell myself it's no use worrying. But pretty soon I'm thinking that maybe if I go on down toward the crik

I might just ketch them up to something, and what a fix I'll have Rachel in then, so she won't be able to deny it she was out there strullin in the bog the other night.

Soon as everyone has started going home I tell Ma and Pa that I'd like to go find Rachel down by the stream, which aint a lie cause that's really what I'm fixin to do. They tell me to change outta my Sunday clothes first and be back home afore supper. I figure that even after changing that leaves me the whole afternoon just for looking, so I go home with them and once I get there I put on one of my older dresses that I think still flatters me, just in case I see David on the way. I tell Ma and Pa I'll be back afore supper. Then I go fast-walking down along the road toward the stable and just along behind it toward the bog.

Stepping in at first I get a little nervous, but then I just think about finding Rachel and David up to something out there. The thought of it keeps me going on through the trees. And pretty soon I'm there at the stream looking around for footprints and listening for noises in the brush, but I don't hear or see nothing that says they might be there. I stand there thinking for a minute what to do.

That's when I decide to go along the crik a little further. I find a footprint over in the mud by the log that goes across. I suspect that might be something, so I cross the log and follow the path to where it turns away left and keeps on going down along the stream's other bank. But if they had just crossed the crik I'm pretty sure I woulda heard them earlier from the other side, and besides that the ground is all wide and open all along the bank. I reckon they probly wouldn't go where someone could see or hearum so easy. So I look a little more around the path thinking maybe they gone off into the woods. That's when I see there's another little path going off to the right, all overgrowed and barely a path at all.

I start on down thataway, wondering if maybe this is the way they usually go, since it don't look like morn two people coulda walked it much. Then I see a little thicket up ahead and I think I might even hear someone moving in the woods. I suspect they might be here, so I crouch down low on the path and sit there listening for a noise.

And sure enough I hear a little more shuffling, out there past the thicket, right where the trees begin to clear a little bit.

I suspect that's a place good as any for them to be up to something, down on this path no one knows about. I stay crouched down and just crawl real slow in the thicket and start looking out and around through the leaves in the clearing.

But what I see aint Rachel and David at all.

It's a lady standing there with her back toward me and her head in a shawl looking down at the ground. I think she might be crying. When she turns her head just a little and I see who it is, I start to feel all cold inside. I even quit breathing for a minute cause I'm not only wondering why she's out here, but also what she might do if she ketches me. I stay so still down there in the leaves, unmoving even when my legs and knees begin to smart and tingle from settin so long.

After what feels like forever she finally moves away from that spot in the ground and turns back toward me and the thicket. I start panicking and trying to find a way that she won't see and know that

I been watching her, but if I move at all she could hear it and ketch me. So I just stay so still there in the thicket, and finally she comes walking over with her shawl pulled tight around her head. I'm settin there shaking as she goes on walking right past me and keeps on going through the bushes back toward the stream. And I sure count myself lucky that she had that shawl on cause I suspect that's what kept her from seeing me outta the corner of her eye, hiding right there in the thicket.

I stay there for a little while just letting my heart slow, thinking how strange it was seeing Rebecca crying there in the woods. I know I can't ask her about it neither, since then she'd know I been there.

I'm not in any mood now to go on looking for Rachel and David out there in the woods. I turn on back toward the crik and find a place there by the wooder where the sun is shining down strong and warm. After awhile I dare say I even start getting a little sleepy, settin out there on the warm sand, the devil grass and cattails like a wall all around me.

Joseph

Much as they talk I just can't get it up to go this morning. As if settin in a hot, drafty room on a rock-hard pew aint bad enough, without listening to the old bag-o-guts rattling on and on. He calls it preaching, but I call it sounding like a bag-o-guts. He calls it salvation but I call it hell.

Prodigal son, my ass. As if folks round here need to keep being told how it just won't do to ever up and leave town. As if our dear employer never got the itch himself.

But I suppose Rebecca'd rather that I save my own soul, and Lord knows I don't got much time left for saving it. So I reckon I'll go next Sunday and sit there and act the proper church-goer, for her sake.

David

I can't explain it how she tries me, how it is I got to runnin out here in the woods when the only thing I wanted was to talk to her. Even now I just can't explain it how she tries me. And she up there arunnin too and looking back every so often, just to make sure I'm still here.

I gotta admit she's a much faster runner than I ever woulda pegged her for a girl. And her hair long and dark down her back and her legs so long and lean there as she runs. As angry as I am at her I can't help feeling a little fun in chasing her, in the two of us out there in the woods and she looking back and smiling just a little, like she's had it in her head the whole time to go and try me and see what I'd do.

By an by I get just close enough behind to hear her breath rushing out hard and fast. Right in the instant that she slows down a little to dart around a tree, I reach out and grab her afore she can get it up to run faster. But even then she's pulling me along, and it gets to a point where I have to dig my heels in and grab the scaly trunk of a passing bull pine just to make us stop. Then we're rolling down on the ground in them crunchy brown needles and I can smell them there by her hair right next to where my face is, all warm and woody and sun-bleached. She's breathing hard still and struggling, but I got both her wrists now up over her head and she's under me there in the woods, just breathing harder than I ever thought she could.

We sit there just like that, not saying anything. There's a look down there on her face that's almost calm. We sit there just looking at each other and I'm holding her wrists up there above her head and she aint even struggling anymore.

It's probly a minute or two like that afore I even get it up to say something.

"Toldya I would," I say.

"I knew it." She's looking right at me. "I knew you would an that's why I ran."

I get to feeling a little uncomfortable all of a sudden. "Well I'm gonna let you go now."

"You oughtn't. You gave me yer word and now you oughtn't."

"What—you just want me to keepya like this?"

"You gave me yer word you would and yaint supposed to go back on yer word once it's been guv to someone."

"Reckon I said I'd do morn that."

She's looking right at me still, just lying there under me unmoving. "Then I spose you gotta do what you promised," she says.

"How do I know you won't run agin."

"Spose you don't. You just gotta see."

"I'll ketch you agin if you do."

"You might."

Something is stirring and moving and swelling all of a sudden so that I have to get up off of her—I just have to get off of her—and stirring still even after I get up and she gets up, and even then she doesn't run but just stands there watching me.

"You could run now," I tell her.

"Spose I could."

I'm looking hard at her and she at me and that something is just stirring and stirring there in the woods between us.

"Reckon I'll have to do it if you don't."

She looks down for a mere second, then back up at me. "Reckon you will."

There's just something so damned determined about her, and everything just stirring out there in the woods so that it's all I can do just to keep on standing there watching her as she starts walking over slowly toward an old fallen log that's nearby, never looking away but just standing there next to it, the whole time waiting and watching me. There's a little sweat on her face from runnin and suddenly I'm starting to breathe fastly again, even though we only been standing for a time.

I gave her my word. And it's true I'm feeling something more than a pick now—though there's some of that too—that she done honey-fogled me and put me up to it.

Pretty soon it occurs to me I got nothing to do it with.

"You wait thare," I tell her.

I know she will even as I start going off just a little in the woods and looking round for a branch or a sapling. Soon enough I find one that'll do and I go up to it and take out my pocket-knife and cut off a thin branch from it, the bark of it still green and sticky and alive. Then I carry that back toward the log where I know she's still standing and waiting for me, with a flush on her face.

We stand there a little longer looking at each

other afore I start walking up right beside her, holding that little branch in my hand, my head just over her shoulder right out there in the woods. And even seeing me holding it she hasn't gotten it up to run. And it's true I gave her my word, sure enough, and she's just standing there watching me knowing full well what's coming.

"Git on over the log."

Afore I can even believe what I've said, she's already knelt down, still looking right at me.

"Bend down."

She does it, sure enough, so that I'm standing there next to her as she waits over the log.

"Face forward."

And right enough she does that, waiting there for me.

I get in place to do it, but suddenly I'm hesitating cause I just can't figure out what it is we're doing. For a minute I stand there with the stick raised and hesitating.

Then she turns her head back around and says, "Well, you gonna or not?"

Something lets go of me then. Suddenly I'm swinging the stick long and low and fast and not even hearing the sound of it, not even sure how many times I swing it afore she starts whimpering there on the log but still not getting it up to try and run, and something just stirring and stirring there in the trees and the woods, just pushing my arm to swing it so that even after I reach down to move her dress out of the way my arm just keeps on going.

I just can't say what it is we're doing. Soon my arm is sore from swinging and there's a little rush between my eyes, even as I see her there bent over the log and the place I was hitting all red and flushed. She's making a long, low noise in her throat that I reckon aint altogether unhappy-sounding.

But after awhile something stronger starts to overwhelm the rush and the fever, and my heart starts up beating just a little slower. I stand there just looking down at her afore I go and throw the branch away. I start coming back to myself and the blood is just buzzing and roaring in my ears. My hands are shaking harder than I ever seen them shake afore. Afore she can even turn her head or get up off the log, I've already started runnin back through the trees toward the churchyard.

I know a place over by the cramberry bog where I don't think she'll try to come and find me, and I stay there for the rest of the day. I don't even leave it to eat or take a piss. Markie's fast asleep when I sneak into bed later through the window and I'm thankful for that in the end.

But even then it's all I can do just to lie there, thinking about the soreness warm and pleasant in my arm, and the low, windy rush of her sighing, and how the blood came and went in my ears like the sea.

Morris

Now it's for the roof. Tom and his boys are just now cutting the bolts and shaving the shingles. Then I reckon we won't have to have logs shipped downstream for quite awhile. Soon it'll be for the window glass and the painting and fitting the pulleys and the belts and the vats and the presses and finally building a coupla small sheds for the drying. Then to get the logging going proper again down the river, with mosta the boys up there sawing and hauling out in the woods and combing the bogs for devil grass afore we can even think about turning a proper load out. It's a long process right enough but I reckon we're getting there now with the canals dug and the walls up and the floorboards laid in and the wheel soon ready for the fitting.

Still the smell gets right under your skin, even with all of us just getting ready for Mister Hawthorne to come on over and survey things, just cleaning up and double-checking it all. Deep down I figure we don't need to worry. We built it true and it'll provide fine.

Emma

Kate decides to drive up after all.

Even as I dread the thought of seeing anyone, I know my sister well enough not to argue. She appears in my kitchen two days later, displaying all the single-mindedness and determination of a swarm. It's something I've never been good at—that decisiveness. I take after our mother.

As we're sitting in the kitchen drinking coffee, I put the photo face up in front of her, right next to her mug where she can see it in the full light of the window. "Mom ever show you this?"

She pushes her small-rimmed glasses up along her nose and holds it out in front her, looking hard at it in the familiar way I've seen her look at puzzling things before.

"Yeah. It's the only photo Nanna ever passed down to Mom. Haven't seen it in ages, though. That's Nanna there, and that's the new car that her dad brought home right after she finished school. Probably the first one our family ever had. God, look at her. She's so young. She looks so much like Mom did before she got sick."

The numbness in my mind stirs, mutters, *Just like you, you worthless piece of shit.*

"Yeah. Mom told me that part. But she never said who the other one is."

Kate points to the faceless pair of arms. "Her? Mom told me years ago, a little before you were born. That's Nanna's older sister. That's our great aunt Abby."

Joshua

I'm jumping down outta the corn crib when I first hear her footsteps athumpin on the dry, dusty road. When I look up and squint through the sun, I can see her runnin down from the woods, her hair all loose and flying over her shoulders and shining in the sun like a halo, spreading out like wings.

"Joshua, hi!" she calls afore she runs right up beside the crib, all breathless and wild. "I need a bagga meal an quick. Rebecca's all sore at me for not gittin it sooner."

I start climbing slow up the short steps of the mill. "Come in then and I reckon I'll git it for you." Down in my foot the pain is just going, but I can't say I aint glad to see her.

"Rebecca says make sure you tie it good and tight," she says, clambering up the steps by my heels like a dog. "An then we two can take the jagger-wagon down."

"You just wait thare and let me do my job,

now," I say, laughing a little. I should probly be mad at her for making me rush but I just can't help it, I'm smiling so wide just seeing her.

Inside I get one-a the rough-spun bags and head on over by the millstone and fill it full with a scoop from the big trough of meal underneath. She waits and watches me fill it.

"You feelin yer foot this marnin?" she asks.

Truth is I'm a little embarrassed to hear her say it. I dint think it looked so obvious. "A bit. But figure I can still do the job good as anyone else."

"Course you can. Reckon not anybody coulda kept up with the millin good as you, specially not after getting caught in that stone. Yer one-a the strongest boys I know."

That makes me blush a little as I tie the sack closed. "Gwan with you. Help me lift this up on the jagger-wagon an bring it down to the starr."

She takes an end of it and we make our way with the sack out to the little wagon by the corn crib and hoist it up onto the bed. Then I go ahead round the front and we both take one of the poles and start going just like that down the road, pulling the meal along. On the way we get to talking some.

"Magine you wish you could be up thare on the river with the resta them," she says, not unkindly.

"Magine I do some. But I make my livin fine just mindin the millstone, and my customers right helpful with the deliveries."

"Think you'll git to pulpin when it's ready?"

"Spose I might, though it suits me fine now to do the millin."

"Darr say I'll miss seein you comin to git the meal."

"Darr say you will. But I'll still be at church."

We're getting closer to the store and by an by I can see Rebecca there through the window, setting and tailoring the leg on a pair-a long underwear. She glances up, sees us coming and walks out to meet us at the door. "Thank you, Joshua, for tendin her," she says with a smile from the doorframe.

"Waren't no bother, mam." I finish unloading the meal and take my toll of the load. "Reckon it'll make a good cornbread. I ground it right fine like yasked."

"Course it will, with you millin it. I darr say we got the finest miller in all the state. Come on now, Rachel, an help me with the dough. We don't wanna stall Joshua now."

"Bye Joshua," she yells from inside, already gone.

"You're good to mind her," Rebecca says softly after she's left. "Lord knows it's hard enough on me."

"Really waren't no trouble, mam."

I tip my hat a little then and start on back down the road with the wagon, my heart up and pounding hard in my chest, a silly old grin stuck on my face. The old pain down in my foot is grinding on and on, and I dare say I almost don't mind it.

Emma

Abigail Anne (Lowell) Cranmer, a longtime resident of Medford, NJ, died peacefully at

I sit there for a good hour or so wondering whether it would be weird for me to try calling one of her daughters. I know it probably would, but that doesn't stop me from looking. After another search, I find that Maggie died four years ago, but Julia's still working in a Bank of America in upstate New York.

Suddenly my hand reaches for my cell phone. It dials the number for the branch. The line rings once, twice, three times. For a moment my mind goes entirely blank—until a polite, tired-sounding voice comes across the line, asking how it can help me. Then I'm suddenly hard-pressed not to give an inappropriate answer. *You could call an ambulance. You could drive me to the nearest psych ward.*

"Um, hi. I'm trying to reach Julia Cranmer."

"She's at lunch. Can I ask who's calling?"

"Um, well, she won't know me, but I think I might be related to her."

A long pause. Then, "I see."

"Could you perhaps just let her know I called? My name is Emma Harris. I live in Boston but I grew up in New York. I'm just trying to learn about my family. I'm just trying to figure some stuff out."

"I'll be sure to let her know, hon. She should be back in an hour."

I give her my number, and after we hang up I sit there waiting with my phone on the table, wondering what the hell I'm doing this for. Every part of me is shaking.

Outside, a dome of clouds hangs low and heavy and gray.

Rebecca

Something's changed these past coupla days. I know the signs. There's a flush on her face like I aint never seen afore. And something in the way she's walking, like every movement is hurting her a little, so slow and careful and planned and not like her at all. When I ask her if she's alright she just nods without saying anything and looks off at something distant none of us can see. Every once in awhile I even ketch her smiling to herself, so that pretty soon I start to wonder if maybe it's finally happened.

Then I start to wonder who the boy is.

Then I start to wonder if he really knows what he's doing.

Abigail's suspicious but I reckon even she don't have a clue. Whole days passing and they don't fight once, hardly even speak to each other at all. The store's so quiet you wouldn't even know they was here mosta the time. I aint never seen its like before.

But I remember the signs, alright.

Hawthorne

I spoke with the foremen this morning to set a date for the ribbon-cutting, one week hence.

We're nearly at the end of the building, and Lord knows they haven't shirked their duty, that it will stand for their children and grandchildren. How impressive it is, the way a town will come together once it has the right guidance—that its citizens might put aside all differences to ensure their own good fortune. For the first time, I dare to imagine streetlamps. A town hall. A post office.

The garden, too, is nearly finished. A couple of the boys too young to help with the building have taken to clearing, plowing and planting the sandy beds. A little late, perhaps, but God willing, next season we'll have a little corn, beets and potatoes—all with the mill still running through the winter by the river, its ice transformed into steam. *A fountain of water springing up into life without end.*

I've sectioned off a patch for Millie's roses. The air appears to be relieving her mood. She sleeps now more than ever since we lost her—a balm to me, that she can know rest. I confront my own despair when she sleeps, fearful of burdening her with my grief.

So we continue on with this great enterprise.

For my wife.

For Cathy.

Millie

Again, the dream that feels like waking.

Let there be light, my husband says, and there is light.

But such a light as I can hardly begin to describe—a mere pinprick hovering in the dark that suddenly, savagely grows, devouring the garden and the village, the trees and the sky, lifting up my flesh and my bones.

The flame is coming from my daughter. She is there in the dream, standing at the edge of the woods, the river of light flowing down from her palms.

In him was life, and that life was the light of all mankind.

I can hear her calling my name.

David

Reckon she'll never talk to me again after that.

That's what I was thinking the whole time I was trying to fall asleep that night, how I hit her and just left her there. How I dint even think to say sorry—how I wasn't even sorry in the end. Not really. But I just knew she'd probly never speak to me again. And I dare say it felt a little like being punched in the gut.

But then at school the next day, she just gives me this look, walking by.

She looks at me fastly from under her eyelids and smiles very softly, so that I get to wondering whether she's really so mad at me after all. Suppose it's true that I shouldn'ta hit her so hard, but it was almost like she was asking me to do it, challenging me like she did. You can't say something like that to a body without expecting to get something out of it. You can't just say that to a man.

But I'm starting to think maybe it dint hurt her so bad in the end, way she's still runnin around in that dress without her shoes on and going off into the bog and jumping up on Abe's bare back whenever Joseph aint watching. Sometimes I even ketch her looking right at me with her eyes wide and open, without any anger in them at all but something a little like wonder, like there's some secret, special thing only the two of us know about.

Just thinking about it brings the stirring back.

Suddenly in the middle of the math lesson I have to ask to go to the outhouse so no one'll know what I'm up to. When I come back she's just looking at me with a little bit of a smile, like she knows why I had to go. I dare say in that moment I suddenly wanna do it all over again, if only for her smirking.

After school I think about maybe trying to talk to her, but by the time I'm outside she's already gone off to the store. So then I think briefly about following her, but I know Rebecca would probably suspect something then.

Pretty soon I see Abigail coming outta the schoolhouse and standing there waiting around for me like she does.

By an by I start to get an idea.

Rachel

I dare say I liked it.

Abigail

I just can't get it up to tell Rebecca.

And now Rachel's acting like she hardly even knows where she is. And Pa up there on the river and Ma at home minding the field and the mule. And David hardly speaking to me at all, even after kissing me afore. I reckon a body gets to feeling kinda lonesome after awhile.

While I'm there working at the store my stomach starts hurting. I ask Rebecca if I can go on home. She gives me a little milk of magnesia and tells me to be careful walking down along the road. As I'm walking the hurting turns into an awful empty feeling, and suddenly I'm sick there right beside the pasture, the milk of magnesia just runnin and spreading all over the road. Joseph is in the pasture and sees me being sick and I'm sure I turn red from the shame of it. When he comes over to me he sees I'm crying and offers me his handkerchief to clean off my face. I offer it back out of politeness but he just says I can keep it.

He sees me the resta the way home and lets Ma know where she's out working in the field that I been sick. Ma helps me change outta my clothes and tucks me in and leaves a little blicky by the bedside.

When I wake up later, the air in the room is cold. I look out the window and see that the sun's begun to set. Ma comes in with a little tea then and feels my forehead, but the sick is mostly gone now. Since I've slept I'm feeling much better, so I ask Ma if I can go outside to see the sun going down. She lets me go but tells me to keep to the yard.

I go on out and sit on the porch in a little patch of sunlight, watching it grow smaller and smaller till there's nothing left but a sliver. In that moment I look up at the road, and I see someone walking down along it toward our house. When I realize it's David— walking so tall and easy like he does—my heart just starts up and pounding there inside me. I go inside and wait beside the door, my blood just runnin and runnin. By an by he turns the corner and starts walking through our yard toward the door. It's all I can do not to run out and meet him, but I know a lady don't act so forward, so I sit tight and wait for him to knock on the door.

He knocks very softly.

I run my fingers through my hair and so slowly open the door.

"David! How nice to see you!"

"Hi Abigail."

"Ma's cookin and Pa'll be home by an by. Youghta stay an eat yer supper here with us."

"Naw, reckon I oughta be gettin home, thanks. But I wanted to ask you somethin."

My heart gets up at that. "Anythin. Anythin at all."

"Could you tell Rachel to come an meet me by the churchyard tomarra after yer both done at the starr?"

My heart stops. "Rachel?"

"Yeah. Be real grateful if you would."

"But, I—well, I spose I will then. If that's what you want me to do."

The smile that lights up his face there in the dark sets a lump burning in my throat. He takes my hand and squeezes it a little—"Thanks, Abigail"— and turns and starts arunnin back across the yard and down the road , like he's in such a hurry to be somewhere else and I was just a stop along the way to something better.

After that I get to feeling a little sick again, so I tell Ma I won't be well for supper and just go and lay on my bed, looking at the ceiling and thinking as the sky grows darker and darker, blue to orange to red. The more I think on things, the more it seems like nothing's making sense no matter how hard I'm trying to puzzle it all out. After a little while just lying there thinking, I find myself looking out across the way to Rachel's house, just watching that candle on the sill and wondering what she's coostering at.

Emma

The voice is warm and deep and sounds just over fifty.

"Emma?"

"Yes!"

"Hello, Emma, this is Julia Cranmer. I was told that you tried to call."

"Yes!"

"Well—can I help you with something? I'm sorry, but I don't really remember—"

"I'm so sorry to bother you and I know this is weird and I'm sorry but I'm trying to learn about my family and I wanted to know if you could help."

"Your family? I can't say I know anyone named Harris." She pauses. I imagine her shuffling through some papers. "It is Harris, isn't it?"

"Yes."

Suddenly I'm struggling to figure out the best way to tell her that I found her through her mother's obituary.

"Are you related to Abigail Cranmer?" I ask.

"I—yes, I am. My mother. She died thirty years ago. How did you—?"

"I'm so sorry. I know this probably seems all wrong. And I'm sorry. But I just—I think she may have been my great aunt, and I'm trying—"

"That can't be possible. My mother was an only child."

"But I found a photo—"

"No. There must be some mistake."

I think maybe I start crying; it's hard to tell. I don't want her to hang up. I just don't know what will happen if she hangs up.

"But my older sister told me her name was Abigail and in the photo she's sitting with my grandmother in a new car and it's from the nineteen-hundreds and my mother's name was Annie and my grandmother's name was Molly and it's there on the back but the other name is all scratched out and I just really need to know who she was—"

" —are you crying? Are you okay?"

"I just really need to know who she was."

"How did you find me?" she asks sharply.

"I—saw your name in the paper."

"How old are you?"

"Twenty-five."

She sighs long and low. "I'm sorry, Emma. This is all so strange and I don't want to upset you. But my mother—she never mentioned—and I never had an aunt, growing up—"

"But her name is scratched out and I think something happened and I just wanted to know—if I could just show it to you—"

Another silence.

"You said Molly was your grandmother's name?" she asks at length.

"Yes. Molly Lowell."

We're breathing hard into our receivers, both of us scared and unsure. I can't help hoping something more is now at stake.

"Well, then, Emma," she finally says, in a resigned way, "I suppose I ought to tell you something. Maybe it'll mean something to you, maybe it won't, but I'm going to tell you and you can decide what to do."

My belly roils. "Ok."

"I have a memory from when I was younger. We were living in Medford—do you know where Medford is? Anyway, my mother and father were having a discussion. An argument, really. And my father, well, there was some trouble, with the marriage, and— God, I can't believe I'm telling you this!—it was real trouble. The kinda thing I didn't know about till later, after I was all grown up and moved out and living in a place of my own. They were together in the end, but my father, for a little while, he was seeing someone else. Another woman. And my mother, when they were fighting, the name she would yell at him was 'Molly'."

Something seizes my gut and suddenly I'm dripping all over the carpet. "Oh God. Oh God."

"Please don't be upset."

"It's ok. I'm ok. I just—" I glance at myself in the mirror, where I can see the veins in my eyelids. "Can I just ask who your father was?"

Very faintly, she answers, "David. David Cranmer."

"Thank you I'm sorry!"

I drop the phone without ending the call and rush into the bathroom, where I'm immediately, loudly, violently ill.

Joseph

Something so sensitive in that girl—you'd think she was always afeareda something. Never seen her that bad afore though. Musta got sick off something she ate.

After I see her back to her ma I figure I might go and pay a visit at the store. Rebecca eyes me as

I walk in and tip my hat. "Uh oh," she says. "Here comes trouble."

"Afternoon, mam. Abby don't seem overly good."

"No, I sent her on home. Darr say she's coming down with flu. What you want now?"

"Be grateful for some-a that coffee. Maybe a slice-a pie."

"Well the beans are right thare in the bag. Help yarself. Pie's hog burry today. You just wait and I'll bring you a piece."

She disappears round into the back room and I hear her ask Rachel to hand her a plate. Then I hear something clatter on the wood floor. Rebecca comes back out with the slice on a cutting board, shaking her head and setting it down on the counter in front of me. "Set down and eat. You know it's better on your back for you to set."

"Yesmam!" I sit on one of the stools there and just watch her moving round behind the counter. "Pie's alright," I tell her. "Not bad. Just alright."

"It is what it is and with the coffee it'll cost you a nickel."

"You tryin to rob me, woman?"

There's a smile deep in them green eyes. "Oh hush. How's your old loper doin today?"

"Arthritic. Frisky as hell."

She snorts at me. "Can't say that don't sound familiar."

I drop a nickle in her palm. "And I can't say I'm surprised Rachel is the way she is, talkin like you do round her."

"Rachel is Rachel and missin her pa. You know how they are that age."

I ketch a little something in her voice. "Why you say that now?"

"Well you member how it was. Fifteen, sixteen, everythin just startin to wake up and not knowin anythin cept it's wakin up."

"Sounds like maybe she gone and ketched herself a buck."

"Reckon so."

"Well don't let it surprise you. She's tall and smart and just a little bit mean. Don't take much morn that. I know."

"Hushup. She'll hear you."

"Hushup yarself. Waxin a lady when I seem to member a whole nother girl just like her, back when I was a boyzee."

"Ah gwan now."

"Lord's honest truth. Turned slummock in the end though. Real sad thing."

I get a flick of her towel for that one.

"You just gwan an finish your slice-a pie an see if I ever sell you another one."

"You know you will. Not a bad pie, I guess. I'd have another but I oughta go an see Abe shod. Thank you, mam. Always."

"So long, poppy."

And at that I tip my hat again and head on out the door toward the smithy.

Kate

She seemed a little better when I went up to see her, but now she won't answer my calls. I don't know what to do. I call Dad up and tell him I'm worried, and Dad says he'll make the drive up from New York in the morning. I call her again after that, even though I know she won't answer. When the beep comes, I leave a message just like all the others.

Dad's coming to see you. I hope you're ok. Just don't—just, please, don't do anything stupid, alright?

It wasn't just the photo, was it?

Fuck, Mom. Why didn't you tell her?

Rachel

After we're done in the store and I've started walking back home along the road, I decide to take off my shoes so my feet can sink in the warm sugar sand, with the sun just now going down and the air growing cold right above my toes. I'm happy going like that for awhile till I get to the turn behind the smithy and I think I hear someone arunnin after me. Sure enough it's Abigail—the little goody-goody. She's all outta breath and coming up behind me, the dusk snapping at her heels.

"What you want."

She stops and stands there breathing hard for a minute. I think maybe she still looks a little sick from afore. And I dare say there's something else in it too, something frantic I'm not sure I like.

"I dint want Rebecca to hear," she gasps.

"Hear what."

"David toll me to tell you an meet him in the churchyard."

Something in my belly gets up at that.

"Tonight?"

"Sundown."

Now!

I look down the road toward the house, thinking how I've still got a little more time afore Pa gets home, though I'll probably use up some of it just getting to the church and then Pa might be sore at me for not making supper.

"He really said now? You better be tellin the truth or I'll slug you."

"He said sundown after we're done at the starr."

"You promise?"

"I sware!"

"What far?"

"Can't rightly see. He just said youghta meet him."

I'm looking and looking down along that road. The sun is just beginning to set there behind us.

"Sounded like he really wanted to see you," she says softly, more to herself than me.

I'm still standing there looking down the road when something just up and flips there again in my belly, and I dare say I made up my mind. I run past her still carrying my shoes cause I can't take the time to put them on. I keep to the lengthening shadows and decide at last to run off the road just a little, going round behind the store and the school so anyone looking won't see me and wonder why I aint going straight home. I keep on past the mill and across the field behind Mister Hawthorne's house and then through the darkening woods where the bull pines are already turning black and scrubby against the sky. Soon I can just make out the grizzled wood fence around the church, the grey gravestones peeking through the trunks and the shadows.

I get so excited that my breathing starts

coming out in short, quick gasps. But even then I don't run up and jump the fence right away. I crouch down behind an old tree trunk and wait there watching through the posts to see him coming. For a little while it's just me out there with the crickets and the bats. Then, as soon as the sun is nearly all the way down, I start to hear a coupla twigs snapping. He slowly steps out into the churchyard right there beyond the fence. Even from where I'm settin I can see that there's something a little bit excited and determined about him too.

More than anything now I want to hop that fence but I make myself stay crouched down there, just watching through the posts as he squints his eyes against the growing dark, looking for me. And on seeing that a little something goes up and down my spine and starts to settle somewhere right in my thighs.

Yes. And no harm making him wait just a little.

Joshua

I was fixing to leave the mill when I saw her creeping by.

Lord knows I won't tell a soul. I don't wanna cause her no trouble.

But can't say I don't wanna follow her a little.

David

I got the feeling maybe she aint coming.

Damn Abigail. She's gone and ruined it. I

shoulda kissed her again. Then she woulda said it like I told her.

The church and the stones are all turning gray and it's getting cold out here in the churchyard, but I just can't make myself leave. I don't even know what it is I'm gonna do when I see her. I don't even know what we'll talk about. Suppose I just wanna see her, is all.

I can hear the crickets going out in the woods. Soon it's got so dark I can't even see the trees past the fence. It looks instead like a wall of shadow or smoke.

I'm starting to shiver standing there behind the church and looking out over the graveyard, but I don't hear a thing that says she's here, so I decide to say her name out loud very softly, just in case she's somewhere in the yard and just hasn't found me waiting for her yet.

"Rachel."

I don't hear a thing except the crickets and somewhere an old dog lugging, a horned owl hooting.

I'm really starting to shiver now. Maybe Abigail told her and she just couldn't come. Or maybe she's sick. Or hurt.

Or maybe she just don't want to. And who would blame her if she dint after the way you gostered her the other day.

Maybe she hates you now and serves you right.

"Rachel."

So cold. Shoulda brunga blanket.

"Rachel."

She aint coming.

"Rachel."

Serves you right. Go home and forget it.

I'm almost out the gate when I finally hear a noise over by the fence: her feet landing on
this side and so lightly moving through the leaves and the grass and stepping between the stones. All I can see is her shadow and a wisp of hair on her shoulders. She stops in front of me and stands there shaking. No—she's laughing.

"What's so damn funny?"

Her voice is giddy-sounding. "I was thare the whole time!"

"Couldn't you see how cold I was gittin?"

"Naw, too dark for seein nothin."

"Well I was gittin cold. An worried."

"Worried bout what."

"Thought maybe you was hurt or somethin."

"I beant hurt."

"Why dint you come then?"

The shadow shrugs. "Jist thought it was funny I guess."

"You shouldn'ta bin hidin like that. You always gotta try me."

"Yeah? What you gon do bout it?"

She says it so sudden and so loud I have to tell her to hush. Even in the dark there I think she might be looking at me just like she did at school afore. And pretty soon it's starting to stir again, just like it did afore.

"Depends. What you want me to do?"

Truth is I already know the answer, but she stands there without saying the thing, without looking at me. I reach out to her a little and soon as I do I done figured it out, the reason I wanted to see her. Reckon I wanna figure out we been up to all this time.

"*Why*, Rachel?" I ask.

The shadow bows its head and looks down at the ground for a minute. "I dunno," it says.

"How can't you know? Yer the one wants me to do it."

At that her eyes snap up to meet mine. I can see the whites of them in the dark.

"You wanna do it too," she says.

More I think on it, the more I reckon it's right what we're saying there in the darkness of the churchyard, the two of us just standing there among the stones and the graves. It's true I can't say why for the life of me. I can't tell her what that stirring means even though I'm sure she can see it there right there under my belt. Realizing that makes me a little embarrassed all of a sudden.

"David."

I stand with my back to her and everything stirring and stirring until I'm not even shaking from the cold anymore but from something else, and even now I don't know what it is. I just can't say what's happening there in the dark.

"I don't want you to leave," she says.

I don't wanna leave neither.

"I think youghta stay."

Guess I oughta.

"Reckon youghta turn around."

Reckon so.

I do, slowly, until her face is right there in front of mine. Then all of a sudden I'm seizing her and kissing her longer and deeper than I ever kissed anyone afore, the stirring just going and going till it's near all I can feel. She don't run or pull away or nothing but stands there with her mouth just parting a little, just making way for me and even pushing back just a little, and I dare say there's a huckleberry taste on her tongue.

Abigail

It's just about killing me. Reckon by the morning it will of done killed me. I don't know where they are and I can't sleep and it's killing me and I suppose they're out there somewhere doing whatever it is they're doing and they don't even know how it kills me and Ma'll come in and find me lying here dead in the morning and she and Pa'll cry and then they'll have to have a funeral. And Reverend Samuel'll stand over me there in the churchyard and I'll be down there alone in the cold sand. Just another ghost no one remembers all alone in the dirt and the dark.

I don't want to. I don't want to. I don't want to.

Emma

My mind is at odds with itself.

Which I suppose is better than the alternative, for now.

I could have stayed on that couch for days. Part of me wanted to, even. But something small and hard and insistent in the back of my mind finally pushed me to get up and call the doctor and ask for an increase. It was a memory of something Mom once said years ago, talking about an episode she'd had: *I lost it, but I didn't lose it completely.*

Karen suggested at our last session that I

start looking for a new hobby to take my mind off Mom and Nanna and the affair, so I watch a couple videos online and try to teach myself how to knit. But with my hands moving mindlessly like that, the only thing left to do is think. That's how, after sitting for a couple hours and drinking a couple glasses of wine, I decide to start looking for David Cranmer.

I find his name listed under a registry of volunteer firemen in Indian Mills, New Jersey, some little nowhere place affectionately referred to as a "hamlet" on every website I come across that mentions it. It appears that David was a long-time resident there, an avid bridge player and champion swimmer, according to his obituary. There's no mention of his wife or any other close family. The whole thing feels distant and odd and out of the way. And safe.

Not to mention that I just called the doctor. I can do anything.

Pretty soon I've found a cheap flight to Atlantic City. I've made a reservation to rent a car that will take me through the Wharton State Forest. I've sent an email to my boss asking for the following weekend off and I've even ended it with a smiley—:)—and at this point I can't tell if it's the meds or the wine but either way I'm *totally* a fan.

I lost it, but I didn't lose it completely.

I only want to know why. I only want to love the world again.

And I'm trying. I'm trying so hard.

Joshua

Hell no! No no no no no no no! Not him! Not that shacklin buck!

I shouldn'ta followed her. Dammit. I shoulda just minded my own business. Shoulda just gone straight home.

The way he's got her pinned there up against the church wall and the way she's pulling him toward her like the two of them are fighting and just can't get it up to get away from one another—and their hands, the places they're going—

I can't watch. I just can't watch it no more.

The old pain is screaming down there in my foot but I just can't stop myself from runnin.

Hawthorne

In preparation for the ribbon-cutting, I've taken the liberty of ordering a keg of apple brandy from Little Pine Mill—what the locals here call "Jersey lightning"—along with some firecrackers and sparklers and sweets for the children. The mules will be brought out for riding and I dare say there may even be a little fiddling and dancing in the evening. Several of the workers are lobbying for a fight as well, something akin to the chaotic matches I hear they sometimes have downriver, but on that I felt it only right to intervene. No doubt they'll hold one anyway, perhaps somewhere in the bog and out of sight—but so long as honest work bolsters morality and they've rightly seen their duties through, I suppose I ought to grant them their leisures.

It should be diverting for Millie to see the progress we've made here. Soon it will be time to set the men to hauling in the grasses, logging and pulping. Already we have a client in Trenton, a fledgling supply company in need of twenty bolts for wrapping and shipping. A steep order, but one which will certainly give us our start.

I imagine that with time we may be able to move on to binder boards and cardstock, and, with God's help, print a book. Wouldn't that be something for a humble bookseller from Philadelphia, to establish a trade out of nothing in the middle of the Barrens, perhaps even a bookstore or a library? To guide this little village out of infancy into adulthood? Imagine her—Cedar Mill, a center of higher learning!

Millie is still troubled by nightmares, claims she has dreams about fire and wakes me with her noise. It calms her somewhat when I tell her that the foremen are taking every possible precaution.

The tomato vines are thriving and the corn is up to my knee. I greet each day with all my hopes renewed.

Joseph

Well, whaddya know. They finally finished the dodblasted thing.

Talking with Henderson over in Harrisville at the fight the other night, he told me the paper mill there is mostly bankrupt. There's even been some talk about an auction. Suspects the whole place'll go over to Mister Wharton soon enough. Don't know if Hawthorne ever got an inkling of it but I dare say it don't bode well for the business. But I suppose it'll keep folks busy here for awhile at least. And I figure the jack that he's shipping in for the cutting'll be better than anything we could've had here given David's mischief afore.

I'm watching Abe out in the pasture and it

looks to me he's getting kinda slow. Has moments where he almost seems to forget what he's doing and stares at a fence-post for awhile. I know the day'll come when I gotta put him down but I'm hoping he can keep it up for just a little longer. A year or two, maybe. If we're lucky.

The Lowell girl's still sick. On my way back from the stable I pass the house and the mother's out there working in the garden. I wave and ask her how's things, though the look on her face hasn't changed for three days. I tell her again she oughta call on the Black Doctor but every time I get the same answer: "Reckon she's just a little tarred out today."

Walking by the gristmill, I ketch sight of Joshua lugging a bagga meal out to his wagon. He's limping morn usual so I go around and grab hold on one-a them bars. Boy really aint no Jesse Johnson. Oughta have a pack mule pulling his jags for him. Reckon for now he'll have to make do with an old man.

"Things gettin pretty excitin round here, wouldn't you say?"

"Spose they are, sir."

I wait for him to keep going but he keeps his mouth shut.

"You goin to the ribbon-cuttin?" I ask.

"I aint fixin to. Darr say I'm gon be ketchin up with the millin after all the meal Rebecca's gon need to stock the starr an make the riz-bread."

"Youghta go, son."

He shrugs and says nothing.

"You goin to see Rebecca now?"

"Yessir. Makin several deliveries today."

"Well I'd stay around but you know my old

bones aint good for any pullin. You take carr-a yarself now."

"Reckon I will, sir. Thank you, sir."

Something's gotten into that boy. I know the signs, alright.

I dare say I might even know who it is.

Rebecca

"Rachel, I want you to tell me the truth now."

"Yesmam."

"Have you taken up with one-a the boys?"

"Nomam."

"You oughta know I aint mad at you. I'm gonna ask you again, but I want you to member the Lord is always watchin. Have you bin seein one-a the boys?"

"Nomam."

Little sneak. I oughta set her straight here and now, if only for her dead ma's sake.

But then I go and ask myself: would I've answered different?

Joseph says not to worry but I wonder what he'd say if he knew the whole truth. John tells us *whoever lives by the truth comes into the light.* And he also says *the truth will set you free.* And truly *where the Spirit of the Lord is, there is freedom.*

I am the way, the truth and the life.

She's wicked and no mistake, and a liar on top of it all.

And yet, *out of the mouths of babes...*

Emma

As soon as I find my seat and stow my bag, my phone rings. I jump when I hear it: the default ringtone flooding the cabin with its commercial, blaring twang. I only answer it out of desperation from the noise. I already know who it is.

"Emma, Dad's in Boston. He's looking for you. Worried sick. What—"

"I'm going to New Jersey," I say, firmly, clicking the seatbelt.

"Where?"

"New Jersey."

There's a long silence, filled with her puzzled breathing. It smacks of distaste. "*Why?*"

"I just have to find something out. Tell Dad I'm ok. I'm taking a little vacation. I need some time."

"He's gonna kill you when you get back, you know."

The deadened voice in my mind emits a little snort: *Ha. If only.*

"Just tell him I'm fine," I say.

"I think he'd rather hear it from you!"

"I can't. Tell him I'm ok, Kate, please? We're about to take off. I can't talk."

"You're scaring us both to death and I swear to God—"

"Bye, Kate."

I shove the phone deep down into the seat pocket in front of me. I feel a sudden, strong urge to cry. All I want now is to sleep, to wake up in a place that's not here, not now.

But as I close my eyes, a voice drifts softly from my right.

"Family?"

The next seat over appears to have taken on a body. I keep my eyes shut and give it a light nod. *There. I've acknowledged you. Now let me sleep.*

It continues. "Lucky. I get to spend a whole week with mine."

I turn toward the window and glare at the clouds through sudden tears, thinking it might be enough to enforce silence. And it almost works. The voice seems to deflate somewhat after that, retreating self-consciously while the hand on the armrest goes on gesturing awkwardly.

Encouraged, I risk a look down toward it. A quick glance. Just once.

Turns out it's a nice hand, actually—the fingers strong and well-proportioned, a vein just visible climbing up the wrist.

And there's another thing, too: in the glass of water next to the hand, a single peanut is floating. Something beneath the numb need to cry begins to stir and crack when I see it. I find myself turning slightly toward this new person, my eyes never quite leaving that peanut. A surge of feeling I can't quite name is bubbling up, strong and forceful.

"Oh yeah?" I say, shakily. "Where?"

"Well, in New Jersey," says the voice with a nervous laugh.

It's a man's voice, a man's laugh. And this feeling—and, oh my god, that *peanut*—

Suddenly my shoulders are shaking with the force of it. As calmly as I can, I point to his hand. "You know," I hear myself saying, hilariously, "you have a peanut in your water."

He glances down. "Oh—yeah. I know. I'm going to throw it out."

"It's a *peanut.*"

"Yeah. Yeah, it is."

The force climbs, bursts, suddenly overflows. A guffaw comes of my mouth that I don't understand, leaving me visibly quaking. I hear myself snorting with laughter. "It's a *peanut!* It's all *alone!* And it's *floating!*"

I can feel him staring at me.

"I mean—it's *funny.* Sorry, but, it's just—it's a *peanut!* In your glass! It's *right there!*"

"Yeah," he says again, warily now. "I know."

"But it's just—it's all alone! It's just one little peanut! It's so tiny! I mean—it's funny, isn't it? Isn't it?"

I can't look at him. My cheeks are wet with tears.

"Oh, my God. I'm sorry. I'm really sorry. I don't really know why I'm laughing. Or crying. Or—it's not like it's your fault, or anything. Not that it would be—your fault—oh God. I'm so sorry."

For a little while we're both silent. Then, slowly, he lets out the breath that he's been holding.

"I mean, it's ok. It is kind of a weird place to find a peanut, I guess."

That's when I look at him. I take in a quiet jaw-line, a thin pair of lips that I realize are moving, are speaking actual words to me.

"Are you alright?" he asks softly, leaning in, low-voiced.

"No. I'm not. Really. I don't even know why I was laughing just now. I think I'm going crazy. I'm going to some stupid little town you've probably never heard of and I couldn't even tell you why."

The corner of his lip turns up slightly. "Funny. Me too."

He offers me the hand beside the peanut in its glass.

"I'm Dan," he says. "Who are you?"

Rachel

Pa's already home when I get back from school. He's got chips of red paint scabbing his arms and crusting up in his hair. He says they're cutting that ribbon tomorrow night at the mill and he's got the afternoon off for resting. At that I suddenly remember what happened with the jack and get a little afeared. But then he mentions that Mister Hawthorne's gonna have some more jack brung in from downriver and that makes me feel better some.

Pa says I should pick out a dress to wear for dancing. I tell him I only got the one good enough and it's the same one I always wear to church. When he hears that he folds me in his arms. He smells like the cedars in the cripple. "It's times like this I really miss your Ma," he says.

I guess I could say I miss her too, but to tell you the truth it was so long ago I hardly even remember her. In the meantime I start to get a little restless as he holds me. Pretty soon I think he ketches on cause he finally lets me go and looks a little abashed at that.

"You gwan now," he says. "Rebecca's waitin on you." He tosses me a penny. "Bring a little soap on your way home."

"I will, Pa," I say, and close the door.

Morris

It's finished.

Lord knows I near got rived myself finishing it.
But I did it for her, Sarah.
And for you.

Rachel

I don't go straight on to the store. I stop across
the way at Abigail's house to see if she's coming out
with me. The little yellowed curtain is drawn in her
window and there aint a sound coming outta her
room.

"Hey Abigail. You dead yit?"

No sound.

"Hey Aaaaabigail."

No sound.

"Alright. Fine. But you better not be playin
hooky or I'll tell Rebecca I saw you and you waren't
even lookin sick no more. Bet yer just fakin it anyway."

No sound.

I'm sure she's probly just got a pick on me
cause this is how she is when she's mad. And I
reckon she's still mad at me about meeting earlier
with David. I aint even told her about the kissing and
everything yet and Lord knows what that might make
her do. I probly shouldn't even tell her about it at all.
If she's really sick, it might just kill her.

I pass Abe in the pasture on the way. When he
sees the carrots I took from Mister Hawthorne's garden
he makes his way over, all gangly-like and lipping at
me. He has a temper with everyone but Joseph and
me and that's why I like to feed him. One time Abigail
went to give him an apple and he laid his ears flat
and tried to bite her. He don't really go for bailey wax
and sugar cubes but he'll come arunnin for some

90

greens and new grass, specially some huckleberries not quite ripe off the bush. I figure it's cause Joseph used to graze him out in the woods afore he up and got the pasture built, and that's how he first got the taste for them.

After the carrots are gone I keep going down past the smithy to the grist mill. I wanna look for Joshua so I can ask him if he's going to the ribbon-cutting. But when I poke my head in he aint there so I guess he's probly out on a delivery. Then I figure it wouldn't hurt to wait around for him some, so I go in and walk a little around the millstone. At one point I even climb up into the loft where it's all wood and dust and cobwebs, but after twenty minutes or so he still hasn't come, so I climb back down and figure I probly oughta be getting on to the store. On the way out I leave my hand-print in the meal and my name wrote underneath, just to let him know I was there looking for him.

Abigail aint at the store when I get there. For a minute I'm tempted to lie to Rebecca and tell her I saw her swimming earlier over in the crik, but truth is there'd be nothing but pure malice in that and she aint done nothing to me since the berries—which I figure dint really turn out so bad in the end—so I hush about it and go through with the dishes and the sweeping and the waiting on the customers just like I always do. Rebecca watches me like a hawk the whole time and I almost wanna ask her what I gone and done wrong. But at the end of the day she's nice to me for a change and she even gives me a little extra of the soap I need to bring home to Pa at no charge.

After Pa's gone and washed himself up, I use the soap nub that's left on my dress for tomorrow and hang it out the window of my bedroom to dry through the night. Pa falls asleep a little early after that and the sun not quite down, so I wonder if I've got a little time to go on out to the churchyard. In the end I decide to risk it since once Pa's asleep he usually stays asleep, especially now since he's been working on that mill for so long and I figure he's probly a little wrung out. I put a pillow under my blanket anyway just in case and climb slowly out the window till my bare feet hit the sugar sand. I almost turn my ankle, but soon enough I'm off runnin to the churchyard, through the shadows and the peepers and the crickets and the late-summer cicadas all humming their three-part song above my head.

Joshua

I saw her go into the mill but I just can't face her so for now I'm hiding out in the corn crib till she leaves.

Sometimes I try and think maybe it was nothing—that they was just trying it out for fun. But then I remember how his hands looked on her and hers on him and there's something about it reminds me how a bee'll grab onto a flower and just cling and move and rub itself there, even when it might hurt the flower a little and the bee can get stuck in the nectar and the petals. You know the bee aint asking why it's gotta have the nectar and the flower aint asking why it wants to bring the bee. All you know is without the two there'd never be a bee or a flower. Just like without the stone there'd never be the flour.

She stays in there for awhile and I start to get worried that it's gonna keep me from the deliveries until I finally catch sight of her coming down the stairs and go off runnin toward the store, her curly hair covering her shoulders like wings. Lucky I made all those deliveries this morning to the store so I don't need to worry about facing her.

When I get back inside and move over toward the millstone, I find her handprint in the big trough of meal underneath, so small and light you'd almost think a ghost or an angel coulda made it. Soon as I so much as breathe on it it's gone.

Daniel

I don't really know what makes me decide to talk to her. As soon as that half-assed crack about my family comes out of my mouth, I suddenly really want to tell her that I'm not normally like this—that I don't usually go around listening to other people's phone conversations or hitting on the random girls I meet on my flights. I'm not one of those people for whom it comes easily, who views fate as a pretense for coming on to someone because he actually believes in it, because it's simple. I know deep down that it's not simple, and that I'm probably, in all likelihood, just being a total dick. In fact, I feel so much like a dick at that moment that I just want to get up and go sit somewhere else and pretend I never saw her.

But then she responds. She laughs and cries at the same time because of a peanut, and I don't know what to do.

There's something about traveling that's disorienting—something I've felt ever since Amy left. It's like a prolonged sense of waking up after dreaming that you've been in some place you thought you left behind a long time ago, the vividness of it hanging on even as the reality filters back in piece by piece, all of it merging to form a whole that's both old and new, familiar and unfamiliar. You recognize the walls of your bedroom, the pillow under your head, the clothing you're wearing, but you still aren't quite sure where it is you've ended up. So you think, *Oh, right, I'm here*—but *here* is no longer the place you thought it was, no longer just the present landscape of your life, blissfully unmoored from its past.

When I realize we're going to the same town, I offer her a ride from the airport. She accepts it with a slow little nod, tells me she can cancel her own reservation. When she turns away to look out the window, it isn't with disgust or regret at what's just happened. It's with tiredness, a resignation. Her hair and her jaw-line, the little vertebrae interlocked in the back of her neck, her two ears sticking out like little white sails: *I'm hurting*, they seem to say. *Aren't you?*

I still don't know what I'm doing, but I suspect I could probably just sit there looking at her. For the rest of the flight. Forever.

For now, it's enough.

David

We're standing up against the church-wall like we do when I notice that her eyes are lighting up like the dawn. Reckon by now I know that look real well, so I stop kissing her and ask her what she's thinking about.

"Hear they're gonna git firecrackers," she says.

"Jack too," I say, nipping her ear.

"We could steal us some."

"Again? After last time? Rachel—"

In the dark she grins wickedly at me. "Naw, I mean a coupla firecrackers. We could lettum off out thare in the bog whare no one would ever hearum."

My belly turns a little at that and I pull away to look hard at her, the brown grass and needles crackling under my feet.

"You really shouldn't," I say—and this time I mean it. I'm not playing one of our games.

Her grin just gets wickeder.

"Really," I say. I'm holding her by her shoulders like I'm gonna shake her. "We shouldn't. We dunno how to do it. They'd probly hear it anyway and then—"

"Bet it aint so hard to do," she says, leaning into me like she does. "Bet you can just lightum and run away and they'll all be too damn busy dancin and drinkin to know. We could do it same time they light off their own so they won't even know the difference. I can even do the lightin, if yer too scard."

She's too playful now, too close.

"You know what they'll do if they git you," I hear myself saying as if from far away.

"No," she says, looking me straight in the eye. "Don't reckon I do."

"Same thing I'd do if it was me'd ketched you."

Her leanness is so familiar to me now, the curve of her body at the small of her back and the fragile little bumps in her spine, sure and real as stones. Slowly, slowly I trace them.

She leans a little harder into me, her breath quick and hot against my ear. "Show me," she says.

So I do.

Abigail

The cicadas are grinding in my head. Make it stop. Make it stop please God make it stop it's so hot and the noise and she aint coming home. Must be past midnight and she still aint home and if it wasn't for the noise I'd go out and try and find them but I can't do nothing now I'm lying here dying.

There's a shadow slouching out there the woods. I know it and I reckon that's what Rebecca went looking for. It's lurking out in the woods and clawing up through the ground to swallow me whole. Climbing up through the roots and up through my head and tearing and tearing like it wants to be born. It's settin there behind my temple waiting. And sometimes there are shimmering lights and wherever I look there's something missing. Ma's face is missing an eye and her head is surrounded by light, looking just like the Lord coming to save me from the shadow.

The noise just grinding and grinding away as I'm looking over at her window. The light flashing, the shadow waiting, and me. Just staring and staring at that little red candle.

Hawthorne

I should have been there. Lord knows I should have been there.

Nothing to be done, they said. Such a fever as this—the only thing left to do is pray.

I prayed. I prayed hard.

But God knows I also should have been there.

Emma

We don't talk much on the flight after that, merely pointing out features on the ground and in the clouds. I'm thankful for the simplicity of our silence, the easy truth of our situation. Here we are, two twenty-somethings sitting side-by-side on a Boeing something-or-other flying into Atlantic City— the perfect destination, maybe, for someone who's falling apart. The coincidence of our destination is not significant, but it's still something I never had to ask for. So I hold it close as the creaky old jet ascends and finally settles somewhere along the beginnings of space. Before falling asleep, I spend a little time wondering if there's really a difference between the frightening and the miraculous.

Time passes and we file out stupidly, just moments ago lifted to near otherworldliness. I wait to come back into my own element, but the sense of the familiar doesn't find me, just lingers somewhere suspended and out of reach. It feels like we're still in some way holding on to one another, still waiting to arrive somewhere, even as we walk through the tunnel and head for the baggage claim. The airport is gray and echoing and humid and there's an overwhelming smell of jet fuel and floor wax. For a brief moment I catch the soft strains of Pink Floyd's "Time" leaking through someone's headphones and feel the pulse in my fingers.

"Wait a second," he says, and we stand there waiting until a black gym bag rolls around and he pulls it off the belt. "What's yours look like?"

"I don't have one."

I can feel him looking at me strangely. I suddenly feel very tired.

"I didn't really plan this out very well," I explain pathetically.

At length he answers, "Well, that's ok." His voice is soft. "It's ok. I guess we can stop on the way if you need anything."

We find a cheap rental car: a bright yellow Ford that makes me smile. We pull out of the airport onto a road flanked by gas stations and farm fields and the occasional sex shop, all bordered by sun-patchy woods.

"I'm driving a little slower than usual," he says, looking sidelong at me, somehow both shy and a little mischievous. "I bet someone would be happy to pull us over in this."

I'm too preoccupied to respond. Coming up on the side of the road is a giant champagne bottle, shellacked white, maybe eighteen feet high. Where the label might once have been there's a message painted sloppily in blood-red acrylic:

SALE
3 FAMILY HOUSE
20' X 80' GARAGE
3+ ACRES
FINANCING AVAILABLE
LAND INCLUDES BOTTLE

It might have struck me as absurd, once. I'm still trying to imagine all the uses one might have for a giant champagne bottle as we turn slowly onto a deeply forested road, completely bound on both sides by scrubby pines and cedars so straight they seem somehow primordial. For miles it's like that, all sand

and sap and silence.

"So, where are we going?" I ask at length, in response to the quiet and the dark.

"Wharton State Forest," he answers, gazing straight ahead at the road. "We'll be home soon."

Rebecca

She comes in wearing her best Sunday dress, hair combed and carefully tied back in a green ribbon. She asks me if I'd like any help bringing the riz-bread and do-ups down to the mill. My first inclination is to ask her who she is and what she's done with Rachel. But then I see her darkened skin and long, lanky limbs and a coupla curls around her face that refuse to stay in place, the ribbon just a tad frayed on the ends. I give her a back-load to carry even though I know she'll probly eat some on the way.

Joseph says I looked like her once. I remember days when it might've been true—one morning by the crik in particular. I suppose it could've been true once that I was her, spending whole days out in the bog and never once thinking that years later I'd be spending whole nights at my board kneading dough. I could've sworn I left that girl behind a long time ago, buried under that oak. But seeing her here, now—

By an by she comes back and her hands are sticky with jam. I put another basket in her arms and tell her to hurry afore they get cold. In that same moment I suddenly want to reach out and touch her hair. I want to take her in my arms and pull her close, to beg her forgiveness, to remind her who I am.

"You look lovely," I tell her as she flies out the door.

Hawthorne

At the snip of my scissor, the ribbon parts like the Red Sea and they all rush through the parting to claim their milk and honey. A fiddle starts up playing Auld Lang Syng right beside the barrels of Jersey lightning. The newly-painted walls appear to be burning, shuddering brightly under a flickering shade of leaves, the sight glorious and radiant and true.

"Three cheers for Cedar Mill, the paper capital of the Pines!"

Heads turn toward Millie when she yells it. She too is gazing at the redness of the walls, the thrown flames fierce against her face. The force of her voice shocks us into silence and stills the brown river. Slowly, they begin to raise their glasses up to meet her. A cheer starts rumbling up through the earth, gathering force.

I swear I could just kiss her right then. Right there on the little wooden platform. Right there in front of them all.

Millie

Last night I stood by and watched him as he burned.

I saw my husband melt away, saw him turn to ash that blew away at my feet.

I stood over his blackening bones, weeping with joy.

Sandra

He tells me he just met her on the flight.

That's what makes me think she might be important. Dan was never the outgoing one, never the loud-mouthed dispenser of bloody knuckles and Indian burns. It was hard enough convincing him to talk to a girl on the school bus if she so much as sat next to him, ruffled him in even the slightest way. Habits like those die hard. I wouldn't have believed he was ready to try again. Not so soon.

She isn't pretty in the same way Amy was. Not very tall, a little pudgy, fragile-looking—like she'd burst into tears if you so much as touched her. She doesn't try to meet my gaze when I speak to her, which is a shame, really. Her eyes are so blue. But I suppose one New Yorker can recognize another.

Over the meatloaf I ask her what brought her here.

"I'm doing some research," she says evasively. "I think I had a relative who lived here."

"Who was he?" Brian asks.

"Well—I don't really know. That's sort of the problem. But I'm pretty sure his last name was Cranmer."

She isn't eating as much as I would have guessed she might.

"Cranmer goes back pretty far round here," says Brian, turning to me. "Don't it, Sandy? Bet Tom would know. Maybe he could help her."

She looks over at Dan with the question already forming in her eyes.

"Our neighbor down the street," he replies between bites of potato. "Tom Cranmer. Janitor over at the middle school."

Something lights up in her immediately at that. "Oh," she says, smiling for the first time since she's arrived here. Then she picks up her table knife with sudden gusto, cuts herself a humongous chunk of meatloaf and stuffs it whole in her mouth.

My son is sitting there watching her, a little smile I haven't seen in months playing around the corner of his mouth.

Joshua

After a slugga jack my foot aint hurting nearly so bad, so I decide to go and have a look at what all the fuss is about.

Walking around the mill, you'd think it took a hundred years to build it. There aint a crooked nail in the place. In school we used to read about the pyramids the old pharaohs built in Egypt but I figure from now on they'll probably just come around and look at the mill.

The vats alone—near a ton to each, I'd guess. You could probly lay down in one of them. And the machine with its belts and its pulleys, so smooth and shining. And the iron smokepipe, so wide and heavy and tall. I thought they woulda screened it but I guess they was all in a rush for Mr. Hawthorne. And who wouldn't be, aworkin out here mid-summer. Reckon the vats'll be my place soon enough and I dare say it'll be nice standing still for a change, just using my arms for the pulping and nooin out on the riverbank.

The whole place smells like cedar and the sweetness of it gets into your skin quick. There's still a layer of dust from all the sawing and cutting but I guess soon it'll be from the bark and the devil grass too, soaking and stirring in the vats till they're just about ready to press it. Won't be the nicest looking stuff in the world but if Mr. Hawthorne's right about things I suppose we'll make some good off it. My foot'll be better for the change, at least.

I aint seen Rachel come over to the cutting yet so I'm actually feeling pretty middling smart. In the event that she does come I don't mind staying in the mill a little while, at least until I decide to go back for more jack. Reckon Joseph saw me take that first slug so I'll have to be real quick about it next time. But maybe he won't mind so much by then, since he gets pretty easy-going after just one slug. Not to mention he and Rebecca sure do talk a lot these days and they'll probly be busy doing that. It's almost enough to make a body wonder.

But I suppose I'll just stay here in the mill a little while longer so long as my foot aint hurting and there's plenty of it to wander.

Strange not to see Rachel yet since I'm pretty sure I saw David standing out there with the others and you'd think the two of them—

Well, anyway.

It's a great thing they gone and built here.

Dare say they oughta screen that smokepipe, though.

Rachel

After I brung the second basket from the store I decide to try and find a good watching spot. I know there's a beaver dam a little way off from the mill and next to it there's a thicket all roofed over with mountain laurel and stickers. I figure no one would think to look for me in a patcha stickers, so I climb over the dam to the other side and then down again so I can sit on the ground there with the thorns and the leaves and the dam all around me, hiding me from anyone who might be looking.

I'm hoping I can see where they put them firecrackers.

Daniel

We're sitting on the olive green sofa in Tom Cranmer's den, an overstuffed, wallpapered room divided from the kitchen by a puckered pane of yellow glass, distorted and smoke-thickened, the kind you sometimes see in old restaurant booths. In the corner is a squarish, rabbit-eared television, on and bright but muted. A rumbling orange cat with a hairless tail is making its rounds, occasionally pushing the boulder of its head into Tom's ankle.

He's wearing a worn Phillies t-shirt and smoking a half-gone cigarette. He's balder now than I remember him being, his scalp shining in the sun as if it were made of water.

"I'll tell you what I remember about Uncle David," he's saying, "though I dare say it won't be much. I wasn't too old myself when he died."

"I'd appreciate anything you could tell me," Emma says.

"He was nice. Always tried to make me laugh. Gave me a rubber band gun once he made himself. I used to shoot my sisters with it."

"Did he always live around here?"

"Far as I know. Told me once he and my dad both grew up in Cedar Mill way out on the Mullica, right next to the wooder. But it's just a ghost town now. We used to go drinking out there in high school but I'm not even sure you can find it anymore. At any rate, he married my Aunt Abby and they settled here for awhile so he could stay close to my dad who was his younger brother. Dad was a lot younger, you see. His name was Mark but they all called him Markie. And Uncle David decided to look out for him till he married my mom and they settled down and had me and my sisters."

"Your uncle never mentioned having a sister-in-law?"

"Nope, just him and Aunt Abby far as I know." He considers her for a minute. "Remind me what it is you're trying to find out again?"

She's quiet, gazing down at her hands. "I'm just trying to learn about my family," she says.

I can just make it out in her at that precise moment: the way she starts to slump a little toward her soft, approaching indifference, how it threatens to pillow in around her, so silent and numbly insistent. It's a feeling I know well. I suddenly feel a strong need to comfort her.

"Emma, Tom's been living here his whole life."

"He's right. They call us Pineys," Tom adds with a smile.

She nods then, straightens, looking briefly at me and then back at Tom. "Is there anything else you remember about him?"

"Nothing too much except he seemed sad a lot. Didn't talk very much. Sometimes spent his evenings alone at the Countryside down the street."

"What do you think happened?"

"Well, I didn't know it then—too young at the time, I guess—but he and my aunt didn't get along too well toward the end. For awhile he was staying with us and my Dad. That's when I remember seeing him the most, when he gave me the rubber band gun. I was only three or four at the time. Found out later it wore on my aunt and my cousins real bad, him staying with us. We never saw him again after that, though Dad said he was finally with my aunt when he died."

"Do you know what broke them apart?"

"Not too sure. Figure maybe another woman. Never met her myself but he and my Dad would fight about it a lot. And Dad would tell him he was wasting his time and Uncle David could never answer to that."

"Was the woman's name Molly?"

She's staring at him intensely now. I wonder briefly if I should have brought her here. But before I can say anything, she declares that Molly Lowell was her grandmother and adds with an awkward, humorless laugh, "Her sister. The other woman."

Tom's eyes get bigger than I thought humanly possible.

"But Aunt Abby—she never—who'd you say your mother was again?"

"Annie. Annie Harris. Her maiden name was Lowell. She was Molly's daughter."

"Her *daughter?*"

Emma nods. "My sister and I never knew our grandfather," she adds quietly.

For a long time no one speaks, the only sound in the room of the purring cat. Eventually I look over at Emma and see that her hands are shaking. Tom is gazing down at the carpet, nodding a little to himself, the understanding growing clear in his expression.

"Well, shit," he says at last, softly and wonderingly. "I guess that makes us family, don't it."

She relaxes visibly. "I guess so."

"Well, shit," he says again. Then he exhales loudly and holds out a hand. "It's nice to finally meet you, Emma Harris. I never knew I had a second cousin."

She takes it carefully; slowly, they shake. "Likewise."

"So, uh—yeah," he says, reaching up to smooth back his scalp. "Wow. Now we got that outta the way, maybe you can tell me what it is you're really out here looking for."

Her entire aspect has changed. She's sitting straight and tall and breathless on the sofa next to me.

"Maybe you could tell us how to get to Cedar Mill," she says.

Joshua

I can just see her over there behind the beaver dam, crouching down under all them stickers and hiding right there by the river.

Right where they just drugged a passel-a barrels.

She starts crawling out slowly, unsticking the thorns from herself and looking around to see if anyone's spying. She aint looking up at the window though. Reckon she aint expecting me to be the one that sees her. Reckon she don't even know I been watching.

She crawls and crouches over by the biggest of the barrels. She wrestles with the lid until it finally gives with a little creak. Figure no one but me'll hear it since the evening's all filled up with crickets and laughter and fiddling.

She reaches in a long, thin arm and pulls out one of the big red firecrackers, thick as the trunk on a young bull pine.

Then she pulls out another one.

And another.

And another.

Abigail

Supposing I did it. Just supposing I did it. It probly aint even hard to carry and no one home to see me since they all gone over to the mill. All I gotta do is reach up to the sill and take it and bring it in the morning with alla them asleep in their beds. I know where Pa keeps the matches in the kitchen and there aint a single breeze so it probly wouldn't even blow out once. *A light shines in the darkness.*

Then the shadow wouldn't come. And David wouldn't have to go work in the mill and I wouldn't go under the ground. And then him and me—

Well. Just supposing I did it, is all.

Emma

Tom spends a little time outside rooting around in the glove compartment of his 1983 Chevy. When he returns, it's with a map he's torn out from an outdated road atlas. He smoothes it out flat on the worn kitchen table and makes an X with a sharpie where he thinks Cedar Mill used to be.

"Probably about a half-hour drive, if I'm remembering it right," he says. "They only scienced the road up to here"—he points to a spot where no road is visible—"but if you keep on going you should hit a pile of charcoal and a bunch of old foundations out there by the river."

For a brief moment Dan looks up knowingly, then down again, mumbles quietly, "Charcoal, huh."

Tom turns to him. "Yeah. All's left of it. Whole place burned down a long time ago. Killed a bunch of the folks living there."

"Damn."

Tom shrugs. "Yeah, well, you know. Funny thing is they never really figured it out. You ask the historians and they'll tell you it was arson. Others think something went wrong with the paper mill they were working on out there. You ask me, though, trees in these woods need fire like most other trees need rain. Everything about them's made to burn—it's the only thing that makes the cones open. So I think it could've been anything. Could've been a falling spark, or a candle, or lightning."

"Somehow I don't think it was lightning," Dan says to himself, darkly.

On the way out the door, Tom hands me a creased photograph—a faded, formal shot of his uncle and aunt, David and Abigail, sitting side by side in two thick, heavy wooden chairs, holding hands across the gap between them. It must have been taken before the affair, I imagine, because they actually look somewhat happy. She looks so much like Nanna and Mom that I almost start to cry.

"You can keep it if you want," Tom remarks then, a little uncomfortably. "I got more than I know what to do with."

The Mullica runs parallel to the wooded road

we take through the forest, separated from us only by a wide patch of dry grass and reeds. Here and there a stand of cedars rears up, dark and knowing. The water is a deep brown, tinged caramel and amber where the sun is able to pierce it. After a little while I ask Dan what's wrong with it.

"Nothing's wrong with it. It's always been like that. It's the cedars and the iron—they leach into the water and turn it brown and acidic. It's mostly sand out here to begin with though, so not much can grow anyway except the pitch pines and sometimes an oak here and there. They call it the Pine Barrens for a reason," he says, looking at me.

"But people live here."

"Yeah," he answers softly. "A lot of people live here."

We pass a few migrant workers' trailers and cranberry bogs, immense pools of scarlet that seem to bubble up out of the ground as if the earth itself were capable of bleeding. Pickers wade through them in tall rubber boots, wielding rakes over the berries, shepherding them in. Then the light grows dim once again as we reenter the forest, the sun eaten by cedars and needly pines. Sandy trails lead off into the sappy green darkness on the shoulders of the road.

At some point I fall asleep, and wake some time later to realize that the road has once again opened slowly before us, letting in a great shaft of sunlight. It blindingly wavers off a sudden sea of devil grass that couches us in fully. Off to the side and clustered together in a large, shady clearing are a couple box-like buildings, dark, wooden-shingled and lichen-covered. Further off, an Italianate-style tower looms over the trees, shocking in its unlikeliness. Further on and closer to the road, there's a visitor's center with large glass windows, flanked on either side by a sandy white driveway and a paved parking lot

"That's Batsto," says Dan, pointing briefly with his chin as we pass. "Used to be a big iron-works there, later a glass factory. Wharton himself lived there after he bought the place."

"The place?"

"Yeah. The forest. Turns out there's a giant aquifer right under us. He wanted to pump water all the way out to Philly but never really got it together." He nods again toward the distant mansion as we pass. "That tower was his idea."

The sun is already lowering and the sky hinting at evening by the time we cross the wider expanse of the Mullica. The surface under the gray steel bridge is dark and swift-moving, choked in spots with decaying pine logs. The air coming in through the window smells like sap and old leaves, a swampy, humid smell of decomposing matter that oddly makes you think of living things. Ours is the only car on the road.

I lean my head against the seat back and close my eyes as we reach the end of the bridge and the pines and cedars open up to swallow us. The car jolts as we transition from pavement to sand.

"Not much farther now," Dan murmurs.

David

I never seen her look so excited.

She jumps the fence and careens into the churchyard so fast her foot near ketches and she stumbles forward a good five feet. I can't help but laugh a little, even though I know deep down she brung the rockets.

I can still just hear them fiddling and yelling off through the trees and over toward the mill.

"Givum to me," I say.

"I can carryum!"

"You don't know what yer doin. Givum to me."

She makes a face but hands them over. Soon as I see what she's been carrying I know she done took the biggest ones in the barrel.

"We're gon ketch hell for this."

"Naw," she says. "No one'll know. We'll go a good long way off so one'll hearum."

"You think they won't seeum? Rockets likethese? Hell, they'll seeum all the way up in New York!"

For a minute she looks up at the northern sky and sighs distractedly. "Reckon one day I could live in New York. Just magine me asettin in one-a them fancy carriages, clip-cloppin on down the road—"

"Darr say you might even pass for a lady."

She scowls at me for that one. "Well I'm gon do it alright."

"Not if they ketch us you won't. Come on, we better git goin."

I start walking and she drags her feet a little after me.

"Well I think yer worryin yarself silly over nethin," she's saying. "They're all dancin an no one's gon carr. I'll even carryum if it'll help yer worryin—"

"No," I say with sudden force, turning round to look her right in the eye, transfixing her there in the dark. "You went and you tookum and now we're gon do it. You just stay bind me an keep quiet."

I lead us on through the dark woods for what feels like miles and miles. Behind me she skips a little and won't stop giggling. I tell her to hush up but soon there's a furious tumbling sound behind me and when I turn around she's just settin there on the ground looking happy as a skunk in a whirlwind.

"What in hell're you doin?"

"Settin."

"Did you go an have summa that jack?"

She pulls herself up against a scaly pine trunk and leans on it, laughing and laughing. "Reckon it's just dark," she says, standing there and smiling to herself in the night.

Lord is she pretty.

"Yer a rotten liar," I say. "I aint waitin on you if you fall again. You'll miss the whole show and it'll just be me takin yer licks again."

She stands there swaying a little, her voice suddenly hilarious and high-sounding. "Haaaa—that was funny."

"Hush yer mouth! Waren't funny at all!"

"Reckon it was."

"Not at all. Come on. Yer getting all mudwalloped."

"Oh no..." she whispers, making her secret face at me.

"Listen, I aint playin. If you wanna light the firecrackers we gotta keep goin."

"Oh, alright. Yer no fun."

"I'll show you fun later. Right now we gotta keep goin."

After awhile we finally come to a clearing

further upriver that I think might just be big enough for launching them. I start going around looking for a coupla good sticks, and soon as I find them I push them down deep into the sand on the bank. We aim the firecrackers out over the water and I hand her a match. Then I pull back a little way, putting a coupla trees between myself and the fuses.

"Make sure you run after you lightum! Don't blow yer hands off!"

There's a quick little spark out there on the bank. I can see her crouching there holding the match, her face dark and lovely in front of the flame she just cast. The fuses ketch with white-hot flashes. In less than a coupla seconds she's there beside me, laughing so happily I almost wanna kiss her right there.

"Git ready," I whisper. "Git ready."

Slowly, slowly the fuses burn down and turn to ash, inch after inch, and the two of us just watching and tense and waiting and breathing.

Then the FLASH, and afore I even know what's happened the firecrackers are gone and zooming up and out over the water, lighting up deep bright brown halos in the river that just keep going out like huge shining fish further and further on till we can't even see them no more; until, so far up and far away that the whole river takes on a brief fiery glow as if it was a canyon filled with red glowing coals, the little distant sparks expand and explode across the sky like anemones, like the branches of a big burning tree. The sound spreads out and slowly ricochets over us, rolling and rolling over the pines and the cedars and briefly I can see her again in that sudden climactic light and her deep green eyes are upturned and wet and soft and full of wonder.

Soon as the sound begins to die over the horizon and that shower of sparks starts curtaining down in blue and green and red, I take her face in my hands.

Daniel

"Try this one," she tells me suddenly.

I turn off sharply onto a white sandy path, nearly missing it completely. At first glance, it appears to be little more than a narrow breach in the scrub that doubles back to the packed-down road. But, looking closely, you can just see a deeper darkness stretching on, a tangled way to walk through the stickers and vines over a bed of sun-warmed needles. I park the car there in the sand and we get out. "Might as well," I say. When I reach for her hand, she takes it.

The ground descends slowly, carrying us down into a dense, dark bog where the smell of cedars is as cloying and heavy as the dark water eddying around their roots. There's an unbroken quietness to the place that makes you think of ghosts, convincing you of something present in the wood and the leaves and the soil that already knows everything about you.

Soon I feel a small tug on my arm and turn back to her. She's stopped walking. She stands there a little behind me, shrinking into herself, not looking at me.

"This feels wrong," she says.

"What?"

"I dunno. Maybe we should just go back and forget it."

"Let's just take a quick look," I say, gently

pulling as she tries to remain still.

"Maybe it'd be better if we didn't try and find it," she says now, a little frantically. "Maybe I should just go home."

"Why?"

"I dunno. It's just—stupid. And it's getting dark. And there's probably nothing there anyway. And maybe we should just leave it alone. And I'm tired. I don't even know what I'm doing out here. I don't even know why we came. I don't even know where we're going."

I rack my brain for the right thing to say, but the only response I can come up with is an honest one. "I don't really know where we're going, either."

We stand there in the growing dusk, watching each other. I can just make out her soft, sad smile in the fading light as she slowly straightens up and steps forward again, toward me.

"No one does, I guess," she says.

After a short time following the path we come to a creek, running low from lack of rain and nearly silent. I step in it before I realize what it is, the metallic-smelling water coloring my shoe-laces. On the far bank the trees appear smaller but no less thick than the cedars for their smallness. The loam beneath is crumbly, hard and black.

"I bet there was a fire here," I say. "The river's just down the road. Maybe it's close."

We cross a rotted oak over the creek and continue down the sandy path through another dark cedar swamp, the trees crowded and close-fitting where the flames seem to have spared them. The sun is already nearly gone, the bog slashed through with residual rays and plankton-like dust motes. By the time we finally reach the clearing, the trees are leaning against the sky like dusky brooms propped up in corners. Several miles away, the top of a radio tower pulses like a heartbeat: red, red, red.

Stretching a little over a mile through the rapidly purpling night, the clearing is a small space grown thick with low blueberry bushes and dry, brown grasses glowing gold against the coming dark. In the dimness I can just make out absences of grass here and there, mapping long rectangular forms in the ground. A crushed Miller can glints in the sand by my foot.

"Foundations," Emma says suddenly, tracing one with a hand in the air. "What do you think happened to them? The ones who weren't killed, I mean."

"Who knows. Some of them probably fled to the other towns, maybe made a new start for themselves in Philly or up in New York. Or, you know, maybe they didn't. No one knows for sure."

"How can no one know? You all still live here."

"Well, it was a long time ago. Things just kinda kept going. You know. People went on with their lives."

"But how do people do that?" she asks, her voice wavering suddenly. "How do they just *go on?* Without knowing?"

I find her hand in the blackness.

"I dunno. I guess the truth is not everyone goes on. The truth is things are happening all over the world that are fucking awful. Things happen to people they never even see coming. They get sick and die and hurt each other and step on each other and they've been doing it forever and no one knows all the reasons why. Some people pretend to know everything because they're scared, but the truth is no one who's actually alive knows everything."

Her fingers tighten around mine. "So what do we do?"

"Well, people still try—you know? They ask questions of what they've been allowed. They learn. They do the best they can with what they have because even if we're alone, we're alone together. A life doesn't start and end with one person. And in the meantime maybe we can go on hoping it's ultimately less about how much we know and more about what we've done with it. Maybe it's little less about the truth and more about the life."

The world has slowly given way to shadows and peepers and crickets, their sound thrumming deep in our bellies. It feels as old as language, as old as feeling and thought.

After a moment she asks, "And is it, do you think?"

All I can do is laugh into the night.

"Hell if I know," I say.

Abigail

I'm feeling my way through the dark, bringing the light.

I'm taking the light so I can destroy the shadow.

I can hear it all around me, in the trees and the earth and the sky, shuffling and dragging itself through the needles and the stickers, the weight so heavy and groaning.

But I'm gonna kill it.

I'm gonna free us all.

Millie

My daughter is approaching. Through the window, I can see her.

Her hair, her shoulders, her feet, her arms parting the branches over the garden. My girl, my Cathy. The fire burning bright in her hand.

Asleep? Dreaming? No, awake and alert to this life.

And my daughter, here, at last. She's come at last to bring me out of this world.

I wave to her, whisper to her. Cathy! I'm here! I'm here! *Furiously, I knock against the window.*

She turns to face me suddenly, as if I've just caught her in the wrong. I can hardly make her out in the dark, the way she quickly lifts her finger to her lips. Hush! *she whispers, her breath like flowing water.* It's alright! I'm not gonna hurt you. I'm just gonna leave you alone now. Stay here.

Slowly she melts away from me, her light warm and soft. It flickers through needles and branches, grows dimmer with distance, slowly makes its way along the riverbank, toward the mill—until it winks out and is gone.

She's going away, she said. Leaving me alone. Stay here.

Can it be that she isn't ready for me?

Can it be that she wants me to live?

Emma

We decide to return in the morning, when it's light.

We find our way back in the growing dark

without getting lost, though we lose the path for part of the way and briefly find ourselves stumbling through a patch of low bushes. By the time we finally reach the road, the sun has gone behind a clump of trees and our clothes are pockmarked in purple.

After we get into the car, we don't drive off right away. We hardly even speak to each other at all. The darkness settles around us like a sheet as I slowly lift my hand up to his lips and he kisses me with an unspoken tenderness.

"Did you find what you were looking for?" he asks.

This time I don't try to question what we're doing or where we're going. I don't ask whether I should leave or kiss, deny or accept, know or not know. I give myself over to kissing, to accepting, to unknowing. I give myself over to life.

Joseph

Not a bad shindig, I gotta admit. I'll give him that. The old blowhard probly couldn't get himself unlost in his own garden let alone all the bogs and woods he's gone and boughten for himself. But one thing's for damn sure: the man sure can throw a good party.

I aint usually one for the perfect love and O-Be-Joyful but even I got a headache this morning that's still lingering after all the coffee and walking down to the stable. Spent most of the evening chatting with Rebecca, even danced a little once or twice. Stayed on till the very end when a coupla fights broke out and Mr. Hawthorne had to break folks up and send them home. Dare say I even came close to kissing her toward the end. Damn near would've too, if something hadn't just drawn her back at that last possible moment, something there in her face that I can't rightly see even after all these years.

I can feel my heart beating right in my temple whenever I glance at the sky. Looks like there's a storm brewing out there over the mill, a dark cloud building itself up. Heard there was a coupla lightning strikes over in New Gretna last night. Probably in for a beating over the next day or two though I dare say the rain would do us good. There's even the smell of it in the air, something big and metallic just starting to wake up and lift its head and roar.

Suppose I better go and get Abe in soon. That thunderhead sure is—

No, not a thunderhead.

Oh Jesus. Oh, sweet Jesus.

Joshua

I knew they shoulda put a cap on that smokepipe and now on the very first day they got it runnin—

Oh God let me find her afore—

I'm runnin down the dusty road over toward the stable and heading for the cripple. My eyes all choked and ash-teary. My breath coming low and hard through smoke. The old pain going and going.

There! A dark silhouette crouching under the cedars, so thin and fragile-looking. Is it—? And coming up there behind her—

"Rachel!"

She turns and looks at me but she aint moving.

Meantime a high little voice in my mind is shrieking, *Turn back! Turn back!*

The same old pain stabbing like a knife down there but I just can't stop myself runnin.

Rachel

I'm settin in the cripple when I first hear the noise.

The deep rumbling under the ground. And everyone arunnin and ayellin and there's a line of people holding blickies and passing them along and everyone frantic and some of them crying too and suddenly it's getting a little hard to breathe and David's down there hauling a full pail over from the crik and starting to pass it down along the line, all sweat and muscle and fear, and the air is fulla bone-grey dust and flakes that are darker and more fragiler than snow.

Over by the edge of the bog something ketches my eye and I think maybe I see Joshua standing there waving his arms. He might be calling out my name but it's hard to hear over all the yelling and crying and shaking in the earth. He's pointing out there past the cedars right behind me, in the direction where all the birds are flying from and suddenly a coupla deer come leaping out right through the huckleberry bushes and Lord they all just look so afeared. Then he starts runnin toward my little cave of trees, limping along on his one bad foot, his rough miller's hands reaching out to me through the blood-red air.

The pine seeds are raining down around us.

Daniel

She starts kissing me softly at first, then harder, and before I know it I'm kissing her back, too, tasting the sudden, intense familiarity of her that's reaching all the way into the root of the hurt still throbbing deep down inside. Soon we're clinging to each other so fiercely and suddenly that I don't think we could let go even if we tried.

I lower my hands to her hips as she slowly climbs on top of me. "You sure?" I ask for both of us.

She looks at me, moves against me slowly and deliberately. "I'm sure," she says. "I want this."

She helps me put on a condom and we start doing it right there in the car, the woods darkening and paling around us until it seems like there's nothing left but the two of us there in the passenger seat, the light on the dash and the sound of our breath and the peepers going on and on in the distance. It isn't like what you see in movies. It's awkward and cramped and there's lots of frantic adjusting. We ride and thrust so fast at one point that her elbow hits the car horn, sending a thick, sharp cry off into the dark.

"*Shit*," she exclaims, tensing all around me.

But as we sit there quietly waiting it out, she makes another sound. She laughs.

We sit there in the front seat in the dark afterward, wrapped up in an old blanket I pulled out of the trunk.

She sits up slowly and looks at me, her blue eyes wide and wondering and open.

"There's something I should tell you," she says.

David

I find her hiding in a crumbling jailhouse oak out by Tom's Folly, crouching low in the pool of stagnant water that probably saved her, gasping and sobbing in the char and the bones and the ash. Her dress is torn and muddy, so singed it's near to falling off her. Her hands are trembling and raw and empty. Her mouth is a dark hole.

It's all I can do to go over there and hold her.

"Hush, Abigail," I say, kissing the top of her sooty head. "Hushup now. I promise. It's gon be ok. They're lookin. They're gonna find her soon."

Emma

And so we ransom ourselves to one another.

Afterward, I find myself looking at his face: the smooth brow, the deep green eyes, the dark brown and slightly curly hair. The face. It's waiting, calm and receptive. It's soft and warm and real, and somehow, miraculously, it's mine.

Over the next hour or so, I tell him everything. I leave nothing out. I don't sugarcoat. I sit there in that dark car out in the middle of nowhere, bleeding words.

Joseph

There's a streak of ash smeared across her face like a child's hand-print and a heightened look in her green eyes that almost reminds me of the girl I used to know, if only she dint look so frightened and strange. "We found im. We found im. We found Joshua," she's saying, her voice stretched high and thin and tight.

"You sure?"

She nods. Her expression says I oughtn't ask anymore about it.

"The girls?"

"The Lowell home was sparred."

I get that feeling again like I got at the ribbon-cutting—that there's something she aint saying—so I wait and wait and wait. At last I have to ask her:

"And Rachel?"

And at that she breathes in sudden and loud, a sharp animal moan that cuts me down deep. It's almost like I hardly ever knew her. I never seen her cry so hard. I never seen her look so helpless.

"I dunno! I dunno! No sign. No body. Nethin. The house is gone. Burnt to the ground. If she was out in the bog, with the Lord's help—"

With seventeen already dead or missing, it's all I can do now to stay standing up.

"Lord've mercy," I hear myself whispering. "Lord've mercy on us."

After another coupla hours searching for the missing in the woods and the ash, I come back to where I got Abe tied up to a little mangled trunk of a tree. He's been singed some but he's already nudging me for his oats. I still can't think how he ever got it up to jump a burning fence but that's how David tells it—and that he let all hell loose bolting through the bucket brigade besides. Funny to think that Hawthorne and his wife were among them, but sure enough they passed the buckets good as anyone else. I must say I almost admired the man. What it must mean to a body, seeing all the work of his hands and soul burn to the ground. I doubt they'll be stayin much longer.

Looking down along the line of ashy stumps where the fence-posts used to be, I see Rebecca coming up the road again. Something about her sets my heart pounding—something in her walk that's stubborn and determined. She's looking me right in the eye. The remaining blackened char of the store is still smoking a little behind her.

She comes up and stands in front of me, taking my hand, her eyes never once leaving mine. "Thare's somethin I think I oughta tell you," she says.

She leads me down the road and around the foundations of the stable, deep through the burnings past the crik where there are still some traces of unleveled woods. She brings me up against the edge of a clearing by a little circle of charred ground. My heart is pounding so hard in my chest that it feels like to burst right out there and tumble on down in the charcoal and the dust. I'm waiting any minute for my foot to bump a little blackened skull.

"His grave is right here." She's pointing down at the ash under a still-smoking fag end of oak.

"Whose grave?" I ask.

"Your son."

Daniel

She falls asleep with her head on my chest, her hair taking on the smell of the car: faux leather mixed with sweat and Suave shampoo.

My thoughts are going in every direction.

First, admittedly, there's *warning*, followed by *crazy, needy, broken.* But then there's also *smart, honest* and *strong*. And in the end, despite what I ever once envisioned for myself or believed to be real and true and perfect, I find myself settling on *trust*.

"You know," I say, "for me, there was someone—"

I get it all out right before we fall asleep. I tell her about those six wasted years of my life, the photos I stumbled on that she had so carefully buried in the bowels of her hard drive: recent photos, images of things I thought she'd only shown to me, images I hadn't taken myself. I let Emma slip into the rough, frizzled, sparking hole inside that's still trying desperately to heal. Slowly, she settles down inside it.

Sometime a little before dawn she lifts her head slowly and looks at me, her hair sticking straight up on one side. Through the window behind her a comforting outline is emerging, familiar branches hovering in a slowly lightening sky. I think of the view from my old bedroom window, suddenly remember that I'm home.

"I just thought of something," she says.
"Yeah?"
"Intelligence. The ability to hold two opposing ideas in mind at the same time while still being able to function. F. Scott Fitzgerald."
"—yeah? What made you think of that?"
She settles down against me with a yawn. "I dunno. I guess it just sounds a lot more like regular living to me."
I suppose I could say something about how we all must be getting smarter, but instead I kiss the top of her head, then her eyes, her nose, her lips. Beneath the weight of her skull I can feel her

pulse going softly in her throat: the warm, imperfect sensation of something fully alive and mortal and human, something deep and rhythmic and strong.

Rebecca

"You know it's the right thing," I say, drawing him close to kiss his forehead. I know that he'll be who he is in my arms.

"Reckon it is," he says very quietly.

"The burns're too severe."

"Reckon they are."

I let him go and slowly he walks over by the tree and grabs hold of the halter, turning the horse round toward an unburnt section of woods where a few of the huckleberry bushes still grow in patches. The poor thing's limping like you wouldn't believe, the holdfasts festered down to the bone.

Joseph picks up his gun where he's leaned it up against the tree trunk.

"Come on, Abe," he says. "Come on, old boy."

Emma

The morning rises like a breath, blue and cold and silent. I wake up couched in the light and his warmth.

My mother is dead.

Climbing out of the car, stiff and stretching, we make our way back to the clearing and the pale, ruined foundations. We immediately find them standing up straight in flickering sun patches, hovering over the sand and the needles and the sphagnum moss, lifting themselves up through cracks in the old lime, each red pouch a vein-covered heart, a flaming pair of lungs filled up with air.

My mother is dead.

"Lady's slipper," Dan says softly. "Wild orchids."

"Rare?"

"Rare enough. The soil has to be right and a bee has to get trapped in the flower—see? There may not be any nectar but it has to trust the smell. And once it climbs in it can only get back out through the top, where the pollen is."

Their smell is insistent and strangely familiar.

My mother is dead and yet.

And yet.

"They're beautiful."

"Yeah," he answers, turning to look at me. "You know, it's funny. We used to call them whippoorwill shoes."

Elizabeth Moore grew up in Indian Mills, New Jersey (population just shy of 6500), not far from the heart of the Pinelands National Reserve. The unique ecology and culture of this region have always had a strong influence on her writing, both poetry and prose. Her work often explores the sometimes beautiful, sometimes tenuous relationships between nature and the human heart, between the wonders of youth and the uncertainties of experience, between past and present-day lives. She currently lives in Massachusetts with her husband, Nathan, where she works in academic publishing. This is her first novel.

This book was published by Alternative Book Press. For more books by exciting new authors, please visit our website at www.alternativebookpress.com

For deals on books like this one, sign up for our email newsletter here: http://eepurl.com/Y_l6n